"Ge

He rose from his seated position and suddenly Frances found herself all too close for comfort. "Admit you're not as independent as you thought," he whispered. "The male superiority thing really has your nerves all a-tingle." He moved nearer, sliding his hands up her arm, holding her captive.

"Get out of my house this instant!" she cried, pointing a trembling finger in the direction of her door. Moistening her lips, she was unprepared as he suddenly swooped down, covering her mouth with his own.

Slowly he began moving her into the bedroom. He murmured, "I think the rest of this evening's a foregone conclusion, hmmmm?"

DIXIE BROWNING

grew up on Hatteras Island; her family has been associated with this region since 1739. She is an accomplished professional artist but thoroughly enjoys her second career, writing.

Dear Reader:

I'd like to take this opportunity to thank you for all your support and encouragement of Silhouette Romances.

Many of you write in regularly, telling us what you like best about Silhouette, which authors are your favorites. This is a tremendous help to us as we strive to publish the best contemporary romances possible.

All the romances from Silhouette Books are for you, so enjoy this book and the many stories to come. I hope you'll continue to share your thoughts with us, and invite you to write to us at the address below:

Karen Solem
Editor-in-Chief
Silhouette Books
P.O. Box 769
New York, N.Y. 10019

DIXIE BROWNING
Island on the Hill

Silhouette Romance

Published by Silhouette Books New York

America's Publisher of Contemporary Romance

For Liz and Randy

SILHOUETTE BOOKS, a Simon & Schuster Division of
GULF & WESTERN CORPORATION
1230 Avenue of the Americas, New York, N.Y. 10020

ISBN: 0-671-57164-8

First Silhouette Books printing July, 1982

10 9 8 7 6 5 4 3 2 1

Chapter One

She knew it; she just *knew* it! It had taken no more than a single look at the tall, earnest young man behind the desk, with his horn-rimmed glasses and his button-down personality . . . one look at the way *he* looked at *her*, and Frances knew she had been offered up on a platter to yet another of Aunt Helen's prospects. After dodging her family's efforts at matchmaking for all these years, she had developed a second sight where men were concerned, but it had been lamentably lacking today. She had marched straight into the office of Combs and Webster, her mind filled with the unbelievable prospect of actually owning her own home, and now, before she could get down to business, there'd be another one of those tedious encounters where she was forced either to make a flat, rude, negative remark or endure an evening of boring company.

Ooooh, Aunt Helen! And after that last one, too . . . the salesman who had actually gone so far as to figure out how much they could save on rent and groceries by moving in together!

The man was on the phone and Frances was gestured into a chair where she seethed as he alternately nodded and grunted into the receiver, his thick glasses hardly obscuring the interest in his eyes as they roamed over her from the tip of her well-shod foot to the crown of her neat, straw-colored chignon. She focused her eyes on a reproduction of a third-rate painting and allowed her mind to go back to three nights ago. She had been having dinner with Aunt Helen and Uncle Jerrold in Durham and the talk had moved around to the old Cairington place on the Haw River.

"I happen to know it's going on the market," Aunt Helen had said, knowing of, though not approving Frances's determination to buy a small house of her own. "The little factor's cottage down by the water, too, I guess. Probably go together. Here, have some more turnip greens, Fancey."

Frances helped herself absently, her mind already engaged in exploring the large yellow house on the hill overlooking the best stretch of white water on the Haw. She remembered the smaller place at the foot of the hill, although it hadn't occurred to her that they were owned by the same person, but as it turned out, they were being sold either separately or together and Aunt Helen just happened to know the realtor who was listing them.

That should have tipped her off—the very fact that Aunt Helen was sending her to see the realtor, when Frances knew very well that every member of her immediate family deplored her determination to live her own life, to own her own home with no help or interference from any man.

And now, here she was, being greeted as if she were the answer to a bachelor's prayer just because she had a good job, a savings account, and was considered attractive enough to offset her uncomfortably independent personality.

Mr. Combs insisted on showing her pictures of his other listings, whether suitable or not, and because she was intent on finding a place well away from the immediate influence of well-meaning friends and relatives, she looked. She looked, that is, until she became aware of his careless brushing against her when he turned the pages. When he began answering her questions with his mouth practically buried in her hair, as if the escaping tendrils had a direct route to her brain, she stood up and planted her hands on her nicely curved hips.

"Look, Mr. Combs . . ."

"Call me Bobbie," he broke in smugly.

"Mr. Combs, I'm interested in the smaller house on the old Cairington property. Is it or is it not for sale separately, and if it is, is it within the limits I mentioned?"

"Well, now, I'm sure we could . . ."

"If it's available I'd like the key, please," she insisted adamantly.

"Oh, well, I'll tell you what, Frances . . . I may call you that since I'm more or less a friend of the family?" he asked ingratiatingly, causing Frances to visualize several dire and painful consequences for her favorite aunt. "Since I'm all through but for one last client, why don't we pick up a picnic basket and take it out to the place? We can look over the house and I can show you all the, ah, advantages of the location, and then we'll have us a little picnic on the river. It'll be the coolest place in Chatham County, I can guarantee you," he added, practically steaming up his glasses at the prospect.

"Thanks so much, Mr. Combs, but I'd really prefer to see it alone," she said dampeningly.

"Oh, but Frances . . . your aunt calls you Fancey," he smirked, "but I don't really know you that well . . . yet." He ignored the danger flags flying in her green eyes and continued with growing enthusiasm. "I've got all the time in the world. I can tell you all about the . . . ah, the heating system! Did you know the place only has wood heat? We can discuss what it'll take to bring it up to bank standards over country ham biscuits and a bottle of Catawba wine."

She winced at the thought and stepped back, only to have him press forward, his eyes finally settling somewhere in the vicinity of her top button which, in deference to the heat, was not the *top* button but the third one down on her tailored blouse. "You can't get a bank loan on a house with only wood heat, you know," he murmured to her cleavage.

"*Mr.* Combs! Do you want to sell the house or don't you? I'm interested in the house, not in your lecherous attentions, and if you want to sell it to me, then climb back over to your side of the desk and stay there! Now, do I get that key, or don't I? There *are* other realtors in North Carolina, you know!"

She got the key. She was ramming it into her capacious white canvas and leather bag as she marched from his office, too angry to look where she was going. There was only one occupant in the small waiting room and it was just her bad luck that his long legs were stretched out, in their immaculately creased pants, across her path. She tripped over a pair of bench-made size elevens and only managed to retain her balance by dint of some fast and fancy footwork, which eroded her temper even further, as did the instinctive knowledge that he had heard every word of what passed in the office beyond.

"You careless lout! Can't you keep your clumsy feet to yourself?" she exclaimed, glaring at the amazed face of the man who had risen and extended a hand to catch her.

She shied away from him as if he were infectious and frowned at him, far too angry to be impressed by the mocking amusement in a pair of deep-set brown eyes.

"Men!" She spat out the word and whirled to go, causing her heavy purse to swing out and strike the doorjamb. Jerking it to her, she clamped it tightly to her overheated body and stomped out the door into the dusty glare of the late afternoon sun. But by the time she reached her car and unlocked it, opening the doors to allow the captured heat to escape, she had all but regained her perspective.

The two she had just left were probably saying, "Women!" in just the same disgusted tone, she acknowledged ruefully; and with just cause. There had been no excuse for her rudeness to a perfect stranger. All right, so he had stretched out his legs across a doorway. With legs that long, one had to put them somewhere, and the offices of Combs and Webster didn't supply all that much square footage.

She grinned as she cut through the campus of the university on her way to the rooming house. Besides, if *he* had been the one making the proposition, she might not have been in that much of a hurry to turn him off. It was never that sort, though, who turned up on her doorstep with some farfetched tale of being a friend of a friend of the family, or the brother of a once-removed cousin of her best friend.

All such *nice* men, too, as her solicitous friends and family assured her, and everyone knew what *nice* men looked like.

Five weeks later the house was hers. There had been warnings and recriminations from her family, of course. They had taken her determination to own her own house as a final surrender to spinsterhood, a fate unknown among the Harris women, all good-looking and conditioned to domesticity and maternity from the time they were given their first tea set and Betsy-Wetsy doll.

It was a relief to get out of town. Chapel Hill was a captivating combination of cosmopolitan and sleepy southern town, small enough during the summer months but full to overflowing during the school year with university students. Frances's rooms had been in a large old Victorian house on a tree-shaded street, but she had felt hemmed in all the same. There was no yard she could call her own and the phone in the hall served them all, as did the noisy old furnace with its voracious appetite for oil.

It was more than that, though. Frances recognized the move as a statement to all concerned. Frances Ann Harris, maiden lady of some twenty-seven winters, is self-sufficient, self-supporting and self-satisfied, thank you, nor has she any intention of washing, cooking, and cleaning for the first man who offers her a roof over her head and a ring on her finger.

She took a week off to move. Her boss, a thoroughly married man who understood her passion for independence, offered to help her with the heavy things, but his wife, who happened to be in the shop at the time, reminded him that he was helping *her* with the freezing and canning and wouldn't have any time left over for fun.

Now, hugging herself gleefully, she stood in her freshly painted yellow living room and glowed with the enormous satisfaction of being surrounded by her very own things in her own house on her own half-acre. The mouse who shared her kitchen was *her* mouse and the clumsy woodwork in the remodeled blue bedroom was *her* clumsy woodwork. A new mother watching her only child's first steps could hardly feel more pride.

The kitchen was hopeless at the moment and Frances's newly revised budget didn't allow much leeway for improvement, not with the mortgage payments and a new floor furnace to pay for. She cooked herself a small steak and opened a bottle of Cabernet Sauvignon as a private housewarming. The public was invited to a modest affair on the weekend; friends and family, plus the inevitable young men who "just happened to be visiting and came along." Her mother still hadn't given up, worst luck!

From the tall, prim window overlooking the hill beyond her came the intrusive sound of a chainsaw and Frances lowered her feet from the coffee table and peered out at the lush woods that surrounded her on two sides: nothing but a pair of doves who were behaving in a shocking manner, and a squirrel working on a winter supply of hickory nuts.

She sauntered to the back door . . . *her* back door, lovely in spite of the bas-relief of countless coats of enamel. Following the sickening whine of the saw, she was just in time to see the top of one of the crepe myrtles that lined the driveway shiver, cascading a shower of rose-colored blossoms to the ground.

Feeling as if her own flesh were being assaulted, she slammed out of the door and down the steps to fly across the lawn, her shoes forgotten and the stemmed wineglass still clutched in her hand.

"You stop that! Leave that tree alone!" she commanded, coming to a breathless halt just as one of the cedars that had insinuated itself between the crepe myrtles and then grown to an enormous size began a slow, solemn descent.

Something struck her in the back, knocking the glass from her fingers, and before she could even cry out, she was sprawling flat out on the ground with a ton of something hot and hard on top of her. For several long moments she could only lie there, the breath knocked from her, as one by one her bruises and abrasions made themselves felt. The combination of rage, windedness, and the heavy weight on her back made it impossible for her to express herself until she felt the weight gingerly removed. Then slowly, cautiously, she rolled over on her back to stare up in stunned outrage at the length of blue denim and bronzed, glistening flesh that towered over her.

"Are you absolutely insane?" she demanded, her words coming softly, with an indignant terseness that tightened up her usual drawl.

A westering sun was behind the head of the individual who stood there with such arrogant unconcern after having tackled her and knocked her down, and she could see only an unlikely expanse of shoulders and a glint of silver high above where she still lay on the ground.

"No, but you must be to go barging under a falling tree like that." The words hung there, bitten off and spat out with disgust, and Frances, still snarled up in the angry brown eyes, put out a hand to ease herself into a sitting position, not caring for the disadvantage of having to look up so far.

"That tree had no business falling," she accused, wincing as her palm touched the ground. She seemed to have made contact with what little bit of gravel still remained on the driveway, which entered the Cairington property from the highway and split to serve both the houses.

"Here, get up off the ground and we'll sort it out. If I'd known any damned fool was apt to come charging out after me screaming like a banshee, I'd have yelled 'timber!' "

" 'Timber!' That's another thing! You've got a fine nerve, coming onto private property and cutting your wood from my driveway! I'll have you know those cedars are privately owned and you can damned well get yourself off this place before I have you up before the law!" She ignored the outstretched hand and levered herself awkwardly off the ground, gasping as she came upright and clutching her rib cage.

"What's wrong, are you hurt? More than your sticky pride, that is?"

He reached out and she jumped back, glaring at the man who looked vaguely familiar. Lord knows there were enough of his sort around, college dropouts or even graduates who had declared themselves to be carpenters or some such, qualifications notwithstanding. Well, if this one thought he was going to do his carpentry with her wood, he was about to be disabused. Besides, he looked old enough to have learned not to go traipsing about on someone else's property with a chainsaw.

Still clutching the place where pain shafted

through her with every indignant breath, she opened her mouth to speak and then closed it again on a moan.

His hands were all over her. The scent of his perspiration in her nostrils mingled with a faint masculine fragrance that was both unfamiliar and exciting, and then she brought herself up with an unladylike oath as she realized where her dazed perceptions were wandering. The fact that his firm touch was going over her with an almost professional thoroughness had nothing to do with it; but when one hand splayed out on her ribs, his fingers digging into the lift of her breast, and he ordered her to take a deep breath, she jerked herself out of his grasp and glared at him.

"Keep your hands to yourself! If I'm injured, you'll be the first to know about it . . . through my lawyer! Now, just pick up your saw and get youself off this property before I . . . !"

"And now you listen to me for a change, you fire-breathing termagant! This just happens to be *my* property, and if I want to cut down the whole damned forest it's nobody's business but my own! Keep your outraged screechings for somebody with earplugs." So saying, he turned away and picked up the mustard-colored chainsaw, pulling the cord with immediate results. The peaceful country atmosphere was ripped wide open by the furious roar, and Frances put her hands over her ears and fled to the sanctuary of her house.

That was the first offense. The second one was maneuvering her into a position where she had no choice but to apologize.

It happened four days later, after she had driven

home, slipped off her shoes, unbuttoned her blouse and dropped down into the dark green porch rocker with a sigh that blew the hair off her damp forehead. It was at least five degrees cooler here on her porch than in Chapel Hill. Part of the reason was psychological, stemming from the sound of the river which was the swiftest section of water in the area, as well as the lacy shade that danced across the cool white side of her modest frame house.

Frances lifted her collar away from her neck to allow the air to circulate while she wondered idly what she could fix for her supper without heating up the kitchen.

There was no warning of his approach until the man appeared at the side of her porch, holding, of all things, a shimmering stem of what appeared to be the finest crystal in his large, well-kept fingers. "This is yours, I believe," he said in a dark, dry voice.

"Mine?" She blinked in confusion.

"It's the same pattern of the shard I carried all over Chapel Hill and Durham trying to match; but if not, you can exchange it."

"I don't understand," she said, and then she did. When she had charged out across the yard the other evening she had been holding her wineglass and it must have landed somewhere in the driveway. "But it was broken, wasn't it?"

"Unfortunately, yes. This is a replacement," he replied urbanely.

Frances bristled, felt around with her bare feet for her shoes and fumbled at the buttons of her blouse. "That wasn't necessary," she said stiffly.

"No, I don't suppose it was, but then, I should have come to warn you before I started cutting. If you're not expecting it, it can be a pretty horrendous noise." He grinned disarmingly then and Frances steeled herself against being charmed.

"You should have come to me and asked permission before even thinking about cutting down one of my cedars," she rebuked and then she recalled his words, words that had been driven out of her head by the nasty roar of his saw. "Did you say . . . You mentioned that you had some connection to the property?" she said hesitantly.

The sun shone down at a low angle, turning his eyes to honey, although there was nothing sweet about his expression. "Look, Miss . . . I'm afraid I don't know your name, but as we're neighbors, we'd better get a few things straight. I own the house on the hill and I'm moving in over the next few days. Cabel McCloud, by the way." His jaw, if anything, grew even more implacable and he set the glass on the floor with a fine disregard for its fragility.

"Frances Harris," she returned, noting almost absently that in spite of a fine dusting of silver in his thick, close-cropped hair (hair that fit his well-shaped head like the fur of a jungle animal), Cabel McCloud was probably a few years under forty. He was probably used to having every female within range panting after that fine physique of his, too, she added witheringly to herself.

"Miss Harris," his nod was all but imperceptible, "for the record, I'm not a sociable neighbor. I'd have snapped up this place of yours just to keep it empty if you hadn't beat me to it, but . . ."

"That was you! In Combs's office that day . . . you tripped me up!" she exclaimed, planting her nylon-clad feet firmly on the floor as she rose in one swift, indignant motion.

"I did not trip you up!" he roared. "Dammit, woman, don't go making me the scapegoat for your own clumsiness! Now, as I was saying, I'm moving in, and before the rainy season starts I plan to open up that driveway so a little air can circulate. Otherwise, it'll stay wet and freeze come winter, and while that might not bother you here on the low road, I don't plan to have to toboggan down the hill. I'll leave your flowering thingamabobs alone, but those cedars will have to go."

Frances was stricken, though determined not to reveal it. "Oh, and I suppose you just happen to have a use for the wood," she said with calculated sweetness.

He looked nonplussed for a moment and it occurred to her that a carpenter, unless he was an awfully successful one, wouldn't be able to buy a two-story, hundred-year-old house in prime condition, plus several acres of river-front property.

"As a matter of fact, I intended to split it with you, although legally I'm entitled to keep the whole works. In fact, legally, I could bulldoze every tree standing and you wouldn't be able to open your mouth about it . . . legally, that is," he added with deliberate sarcasm. "You bought the half-acre plot this shack sits on and you have right-of-way in from the highway, but just keep in mind that every time you drive in or out, you're doing so only with my permission."

She caught her breath as the impact of his words hit her, taking away that fine freedom, the feeling of being queen of all she surveyed, but as she stared helplessly into his mocking eyes, all she could think to say was, "It's not a shack!"

"Mill house, farm manager's house, whatever,"

he said disparagingly, "just keep in mind what I said. And Miss Harris, while we're at it, we may as well lay the cards on the table. Just so you don't get any ideas about being too neighborly, I'm a bachelor, Miss Harris . . . by choice. I am *not* fond of women who offer to cook meals for me, nor do I need any buttons sewn on. And if my house needs cleaning, then I'll have a housekeeper in. I am not lonely, nor am I pining away from a broken heart. As far as I'm concerned, women are welcome in my bed, but not in my life. Is that clear enough for you?"

Under the apricot tan she had acquired so easily, Frances could almost feel the color drain from her face as the impact of his words struck her. That *he* should think *she* was interested in trapping *him!* "Mr. McCloud, allow me to lay my own cards on the table. I happen to be twenty-seven years old and single . . . by choice," she stressed. "I am perfectly able to change a tire and replace a fuse. I can chop my own wood and shovel snow, and if you happen to hear hysterical laughter floating up the hill on a summer breeze, don't be alarmed; it will only be me, expressing my heartfelt thanks for having escaped from all the overbearing, egotistical, self-important males who think every female they meet is after their scalp. And as far as you, personally, are concerned, why I'd rather send for a man from a mail-order catalog!"

There was more jammed up in her seething brain but her tongue proved to be the bottleneck. She fumed impotently and settled for blowing an irritating tendril of hair off her forehead as her breasts heaved in exasperation.

Then, with a sigh that (had she been in any frame of mind to notice) drew Cabel McCloud's eyes from her flushed cheeks to her agitated breasts, she forced herself to continue on another tack. "I owe you an apology for the other day. You were right about the driveway and even if you weren't, the land, as you so kindly informed me, belongs to you and I only use it on sufferance. As for this," she leaned over and lifted the delicate stemware from the porch floor, tilting it to catch the coppery rays of the sun, "it wasn't necessary for you to replace it since we've both agreed that I was at fault . . . well, if not actually at fault, then . . . ah . . . wrong in my . . . my accusations." She was growing uncomfortable under the level gaze; something about the man got under her skin the first time she had ever seen him and he didn't improve on further acquaintance. "At any rate," she finished in a rush, "it would make me feel better if you'd return it and get your money back." She held it out to him and he glanced at it, not bothering to relieve her of it—to her acute embarrassment. Finally she let her arm fall again.

"But then, I've no particular wish to make you feel better, Miss Harris. You can repay me for the privilege of sharpening your tongue on my hide by taking the blasted thing, since I spent the best part of a morning locating it." His eyes dropped momentarily to an all but invisible line between his thumb and forefinger. "Not to mention cutting myself on the piece I took along to match."

"Oh, that's just too bad, Mr. McCloud," she cooed, shamelessly enjoying the chance to rile him. "If you'll come in I'll bandage it up for you and make it all better."

"Don't try playing the flirt with me, Miss Harris," he retorted with blistering mockery. "It's an art that has to be learned young to be effective and it's a little

21

late for you to be trying it out." He turned and strode off up the hill. Frances's fingers tightened around the stem as if she'd like to throw it after him, but instead, her lips curved into a reluctant grin and she found herself laughing aloud for no good reason at all.

Chapter Two

After living and working in the area for five years, ever since graduating from the university, Frances had settled into a full and satisfying routine. Her social life was well under control and she meant to keep it that way in spite of all the machinations of those who thought a woman incomplete without a man permanently attached. She had almost been caught in that trap once, during her senior year, and she considered the end of that relationship a deliverance, an escape.

Now she did. At the time, she hadn't felt quite so fortunate, but it had been a long time since she had even thought of the man who had come on so strongly, almost convincing her that unless she moved into the house he owned just west of Carrboro, his life would be severely blighted. He had hinted at marriage, but before he could do more than hint, Frances had discovered that since his mother, with whom he had lived, had died two and a half years before, he had lived with three different girls, and the last one had got tired of being an unpaid and unwed housekeeper and moved out. That had been just about two weeks before Mike had widened his eyes over a stein of beer and crossed the floor to drop into the seat opposite Frances with an implausible tale about recognizing her from some previous life.

Chapel Hill was like that. In spite of the seasonal influx of students, a good number of whom stayed on long after graduation, it was essentially a small town where all circles overlapped and sooner or later, everyone knew everyone else's business.

Which was why it was so infernally easy for her mother and her two married sisters to shuffle their acquaintances and come up with a perfectly reasonable excuse to direct one man after another into her pathway.

Probably she should have moved clean out of the state. Bynum wasn't all that far from where her widowed mother lived in Saxapahaw, and with a sister living on a tobacco farm in Moore County and another at Eli Whitney, plus Aunt Helen in Durham, she was still their favorite charity. Send poor Frances a man; she's still wary after that Mike fellow, but she's bound to settle for someone else sooner or later.

If she had feared for her privacy as far as her neighbor was concerned, however, she needn't have worried. She was left strictly alone to potter about her four rooms, two porches, a bath, and a half-acre of weeds which, when properly mowed, resembled a lawn nearly enough to satisfy all but the most fastidious. She took great pleasure in rearranging

her few fine pieces of furniture so that the thrift shop
and yard sale items weren't too obvious. She turned
down several dates, using the excuse of getting
settled and then turned down a few offers to help
with that chore.

About the only one of her circle who didn't keep
trying to mate her up with all the leftover males of
his acquaintance was her boss, Howard Stinson, who
only cast her a resigned sort of look when she harped
overly long on the subject of blessed singleness. He
understood and sympathized; you're a short time
single and a long time married, she had heard him
say once over the phone. To one of his single friends,
she presumed. He was either warning or commiser-
ating.

She didn't see very much of her neighbor but that
wasn't to say she wasn't aware of his presence. There
evolved a more or less regular schedule of visitations
and Frances happened to be on her front porch or at
a window as often as not when McCloud's girl
friends came to see him. The redhead, a real knockout who flashed up the drive in a yellow Spitfire
about six o'clock at least three evenings a week,
usually brought a picnic basket with her, and the two
of them had to pass right by Frances's house to reach
the clearing on the riverbank, where they proceeded
to enjoy the fried chicken and wine as well as a little
necking. If they insisted on settling down right in
front of her porch, she didn't see why she should be
forced to stay inside, and so she turned her back to
the river, propped her feet up on the window sill,
and rocked while she cooled off and read the *Advocate*. Her gaze *might* have strayed occasionally to the
couple on the blanket and Cabel McCloud *might*
have caught her eye once or twice, but there was
certainly nothing deliberate about it. Even if it

appeared to her that he actually winked at her now and then, it was too far to be sure.

Her own dates usually came to pick her up at her house, although sometimes she met them in town for a drink at Crook's Corner and a film, or some live music at one or another of the bars. One or two of them hinted rather strongly that they would have preferred an evening at home, but Frances wasn't falling for that one; a home cooked meal and then all the reasons why it would be better to stay over than drive back to town so late.

Her own social life was every bit as satisfying as Cabel McCloud's seemed to be, even though he seemed satisfied with one or two partners instead of the half a dozen or so that Frances juggled. There was the pharmacist who was divorced and made no bones about the fact that he was looking for a stepmother for his six-year-old daughter. Frances enjoyed seeing him once every week or so because they both had a passion for Greek food and wine. Then there was the grad student who was a cousin of one of her brothers-in-law. He was a wonderful dancer and an entertaining companion at parties. There were others, and if they still stuck after finding out that she didn't lend money or records, that she didn't patch jeans or darn socks, and she didn't sleep around, then she was perfectly willing to see them on a regular basis, paying her own way and understanding when another female came along who promised more than Frances was willing to deliver.

It was the paying of her own way that cut into her social life more than the lack of suitable partners, for with a mortgage to consider and a newly installed floor furnace—necessary before any bank would lend her money to buy her house—there didn't seem to be much left over for fun these days. And then there were the little extras she couldn't resist, such as the swing for her front porch and the bentwood rocker for the living room. And the habit of regular meals.

Tossing herself a chef's salad one Friday afternoon after work, she could hear the sound of Cabel's redhead coming from the riverside picnic site. His soft baritone didn't carry, but the girl's shrill laughter rang out so often that Frances wondered wryly if he were telling jokes or tickling her. From the looks of the clouds rolling up over the treetops, he'd better be paying less attention to his little playmate and more to the weather, she decided. While Mr. McCloud might be able to take a sudden squall in stride, his girl friend looked the sort to come apart at the seams with the first drop of rain.

Not that Frances had been spying on them, but those eyelashes looked far too thick, long, and black to go with the bouffant copper hair, and if that knit top shrunk half an inch, she could be held for indecent exposure. Even from here, it was impossible to miss all that overstated sex appeal, and when little Red flapped those lashes up at Cabel, Frances could almost feel the breeze from where she sat munching her raw broccoli.

And of course, manlike, he lapped it up! For a misogynist, Cabel McCloud had a way of rationalizing his lapses. But then he hadn't exactly said he hated women, had he? It was marriage he distrusted. She wondered disparagingly what the two of them shared besides the picnic basket.

When the first big drops struck the side windows, Frances put down her salad and dashed out to gather up her laundry from the line. She had fallen into the habit of doing her washing Thursday nights and hanging it out Friday morning before work, and she was lucky this time that the rain had held off. If it had come any earlier, she'd have had it all to do over. The rain was upon her as she crammed the last pair of nylon bikini briefs into her basket, and she ran for the back door, shouldering it open just as she heard Cabel call out from the front. The scent of rain on parched earth was strong in her nostrils as she called out for him to come in.

"Through here," she panted breathlessly, planking her basket down on the table that served as work surface and dining table until she could afford to have more cabinets built in her kitchen.

It was the first time he had been in her house, and she couldn't help but think how his shoulders dwarfed the dimensions of the room. Not only did his physique fill the doorway, but his personality seemed to overflow, crowding her against the table as he entered with his redheaded friend hovering behind him.

As Frances looked beyond him, she felt a peculiar shaft of sympathy. As she had half expected, the poor girl hadn't fared very well in the weather. Not only had her mascara run and given her the look of a sad raccoon, but her hair was coming unglued and now looked more like a brillo pad than anything else.

"Why don't I show you where you can dry off," Frances suggested, sidling past the bulk of Cabel McCloud. "I'm Frances Harris."

"Sorry, Frances. This is Terri Bollich. Terri works with the firm," Cabel said, making himself at home by hooking a chair over and straddling it.

Not bothering to reply, Frances ushered the girl into the spare bedroom, showing her the bath and handing her a towel. What firm? she wondered. The few times they had come into contact with each other she and her neighbor had cautiously avoided anything that could be construed as personal, and so she had no idea what he did for a living. All she knew was that he left the house about half an hour before she did in the morning driving a maroon 450 SL, and he wore suits that discreetly shouted their exclusive origins.

"You're welcome to anything you need," she told Terri Bollich. "I can lend you something dry to wear if you'd like, although . . ." she broke off, looking doubtfully at the girl who couldn't be more than five-feet-three or four and who was built like a roller coaster. Frances herself stood five-feet-seven in her stocking feet, and while she wasn't exactly unendowed, her figure was a little more restrained.

"Thanks, but Cabel will lend me his shirt," Terri said, speaking for the first time in her little-girl whisper.

Frances left her to it and returned to the kitchen to collect the basket of rain-dampened clothes. Through the windows she could see the fronds of ailanthus tossing in the gray sheets of rain like palm trees in a hurricane as the fury on her tin roof almost deafened her.

"Thanks for the shelter," Cabel remarked laconically, leaning over to sweep up a pair of wispy ivory panties from the floor and drop them on her basket.

Tight-lipped, she stuffed the intimate garment under her more prosaic jeans. "You're perfectly welcome to stay as long as you need to. I have things to do in the bedroom and you can finish your picnic here if you want to."

"You'll have to share it with us," Cabel invited politely. "I insist, Frances. After all, it's the least we can do after we barged in on you uninvited."

"No thank you, Mr. McCloud," she answered stiffly. She could smell the scent of sun-dried laundry mingling with some masculine fragrance that seemed to invade the sanctuary of her small kitchen, turning it into something unfamiliar, and she needed to escape. "If you . . ."

She was interrupted by a click-click sound, and almost immediately a blast of thunder seemed to lift the house off its foundation. Thunder storms were her own particular *bête noire*, although she had successfully hidden the fact for years, and now Frances stood paralyzed as the color drained from her face and she struggled to get her breath again. Her fingers clutched the laundry basket as if it were a life preserver and when Cabel's voice filtered through her consciousness, it was several long moments before she could take in his words.

"Frances! Are you all right? What is it, girl?" He had moved swiftly to her side, coming up from the chair in a single lithe movement, and she blinked and forced a smile to her stiff lips, one that didn't convince anyone of anything.

"Just . . . just startled, that's all," she assured him shakily. "That one was close."

His arms came around her, and for just a fraction of an instant, she allowed herself the inestimable comfort of burrowing into his chest, drawing from the tough strength of him, and then she stiffened away and picked up her basket from where she had dumped it on the table. She turned away and bumped the basket on the door frame, muttering some excuse or another under her breath in her haste to get away before the next blast. With Cabel's terse voice in her ears above the steady rumble of thunder, she slammed her bedroom door closed as if the hounds of hell were on her heels and leaned against it.

"Frances! Open this door!" He was just on the other side and Frances struggled to overcome a hysterical giggle that rose in her throat. Fat chance she'd have of maintaining her pose of independence if he discovered she fell apart at a silly little summer storm. She could take spiders and snakes and things that go bump in the night, but a close encounter with thunder and lightning was her undoing. Aware of his nearness just on the other side of her door, she crossed silently and scuttled to the center of her bed, carefully avoiding the thought of all the metal bed-springs beneath her. One of these days I'm going to read a really good scientific book about lightning, she promised herself, and then I won't be worrying about bedsprings and running water and tall trees.

The bubble of mirth erupted when she heard Terri's husky little cry outside her room. "Oh, Cabel, I'm just scared to death of all this lightning. Come sit on the couch with me till it's over, will you?"

If anything could cure her terror, that came close, and she relaxed somewhat and stretched out on her bed while the celestial bowling match passed over her head and continued on downriver, telling herself that if anything got hit, it would be the house on the hill, not the one in the hollow.

If there had been a way to get to the kitchen without having to go through the living room, she'd have done it. As it was, she settled for making as much noise as she could, and she avoided looking at where the two of them still sat on her sofa, with Cabel's arm across Terri's shoulder. It was none of her business if they wanted a cuddling session

. . . within the bounds of decency, she amended, as she averted her face and hurried through to the kitchen. In spite of her precautions to avoid embarrassing the couple, she couldn't help see the look of concern Cabel sent her way.

Did he think she was offended, for goodness sake? She was no prude! She scraped the remains of a perfectly good salad in the garbage and rinsed the bowl under the faucet, managing to splash her denim skirt in the process. It was certainly no business of hers if they wanted to . . .

She whirled around on hearing someone enter the kitchen and dropped the paring knife she was washing. "Why don't you watch where you're going?" she demanded illogically. She bent over to retrieve the knife at the same time he did, and their heads met forcefully.

"Oh, good Lord, why can't you leave me alone," she groaned, backing up while she felt her forehead for damage.

"You're falling to pieces," Cabel accused, clamping a steadying hand on her upper arm to swing her around to the light of the window. He examined her face minutely. "Head still intact but nerves gone to pot," he diagnosed, and she couldn't keep a grin from trembling on her lips.

He answered it with one of his own and Frances thought it unfair for a man to have a dimple in one cheek while she had no such adornment. Far more effective than a matching pair, too, for it gave him a rakish sort of air that counteracted the sobering effect of his lightly silvered hair.

"Cab–el–l–l," Terri wailed from the living room. "I'm cold. Can't we go now?"

"Terri's cold, Cabel," Frances repeated with mock

concern. "Surely you didn't refuse to give the poor girl the shirt off your back?"

She had forgotten the hand on her arm and now it tightened unmercifully as its owner shook her wrathfully. "Don't get smart with me, Miss Harris, or I might think you're jealous," he said with an outrageous gleam in his wicked eyes. "I've always heard frustration was a problem with women who were left too long to wither on the vine."

If it hadn't been for that gleam, Frances would have brained him, but something about the man, some imp of mischief that belied the aggressive thrust of his jaw, touched an answering chord in her, and she bit her bottom lip to keep it from giving her away.

"Cabel!" came the petulant cry from behind them. "I want to go now. Your house is ever so much more comfy."

"Say 'Thank you' to Miss Harris for her hospitality, Terri," Cabel prompted, and Frances thought that if he were hers, she'd tell him a thing or so. The insufferable male animal!

She smiled at the poor washed-out-looking girl with a mixture of sympathy and amusement, neither of which was reciprocated.

For the next few days her employer, Howard Stinson, seemed preoccupied and was out of the shop as often as he was in. That left Frances in charge of handling the incoming stock as well as serving the few customers who found their way to the small import shop, for the girl who worked there during the school year, when they did most of their business, wouldn't be starting for several weeks yet. Margaret Shober, the bookkeeper, a housewife whose husband had left her for greener and younger pastures, came in from nine to one, and Frances listened to her complaining that unless they did some reordering soon, by the time their peak season rolled around, there'd be nothing left to sell. That wasn't Frances's responsibility, though. Mr. Stinson did the ordering, although he had promised Frances when she had first come to work there that once she got the hang of things, she might occasionally go on a buying trip.

During the middle of the week they were adopted by a ridiculous stray cat who wouldn't take no for an answer, and Frances fell in love with the waif. She —they were always females, needing an expensive trip to a vet to make them sociably acceptable —was three-legged and extremely pregnant. When Margaret declared she couldn't take care of so much as another houseplant, Frances took the poor thing home with her, fleas, incipient kittens and all. Tripod rewarded her by following her around to stroke her leg at every step while quivering her bushy tail in ecstasy.

Tripod had been in residence about a week when Cabel brought home his dog. Frances first knew of the addition to the hill when Tripod came flying across the porch, her black and orange fur on end and a wild light in her yellow eyes. Close on her heels came an even more pregnant tricolored English setter, ears flapping in anticipation as she took off into the woods after the cat.

"Cabel!" Frances yelled around the corner of her house to the tall, jeans-clad man who came swinging lithely down the hill with a leash and collar in his hand. "Is that creature yours?"

"If you mean Mollie, then yes. What's all the ruckus? She took off as if you were handing out spare ribs at your kitchen door." He grinned easily and leaped up onto the porch to tower over her.

Frances glared at him, her hands planted firmly on her hips. "Your dog is chasing my cat," she accused. "What are you going to do about it?"

Dark, bushy brows lifted over innocent brown eyes. "I didn't even know you had a cat."

"Well, I do, and what's more she's pregnant and it doesn't do her a bit of good to be . . ."

The thought struck them both at the same instant, and they stared at each other and then crumpled into laughter. Frances howled until tears streaked her cheeks and Cabel leaned helplessly against the side of the house, wiping his eyes as he subsided into a few helpless gasps. "Good Lord, can you picture it? The two of them are probably out there in the woods right now comparing notes on . . ."

"On pickles and ice cream and the horrible habits of footloose males," Frances filled in for him, breathing deeply in an effort to steady herself. She dropped down into the rocker and Cabel took the swing, and they smiled at each other for several moments before Frances caught herself up and started to babble to cover an unexpected feeling of awkwardness. "Mine was a stray. She showed up at the shop last week, and we were afraid of getting fleas in the stock and so I brought her home with me."

"So was mine . . . a stray, that is. Friend of mine's a vet and someone dropped the poor wretch off with a note to find her a home, so I got stuck."

They discussed the fruits of their respective pets' labors and Cabel suggested some of Frances's boyfriends might be interested in a pup who was at least half bird-dog.

"Some of your girl friends might want a kitten.

There's bound to be at least one orange one in the litter that would match Terri's hair. Maybe she could train it to ride with her in the Spitfire."

"You're a wicked woman, Frances Harris," Cabel chided softly.

"Indeed I am, Cabel McCloud, and you'd better not forget it."

"I'm not likely to," he promised. "I wonder . . . just how far does your wickedness extend?" he mused, slanting her a provocative glance from beneath lazy lids.

"You aren't likely to find out," she answered shortly, irritated to discover herself coloring. To hide her embarrassment, she turned to the edge of the porch and called her cat, adding a whistle for the dog, as well. Funny how she couldn't be around the man for more than five minutes without getting flustered. If he didn't say something outrageous, why then did he look at her in such a way that she bridled like a fifteen-year-old, which was ridiculous, considering her age and experience.

The kittens arrived a week after Cabel's pups and Frances wondered how she could bear to give the darlings away. There were two grays and an orange, which she promptly named Terri. She had counted on giving at least one cat to Mr. Stinson, who had four children under high-school age, but he seemed so morose lately she didn't know how to bring up the subject.

Her oldest sister, Kay, who had married a veterinarian and lived at Eli Whitney, called to say that she had a friend she'd like Frances to meet, and wouldn't she like to come to dinner one night next week.

Frances made an excuse, as she did when Aunt

Helen called from Durham about a nephew of Uncle Jerrold's, who, of course, wasn't a blood relative and was an awfully lonely young man who had come to Duke to do something concerning computers.

"Aunt Helen, I'm really not in the mood at the moment. Work's getting into the busy season, and there's the house, and I've a litter of kittens to get rid of." As if any of those things would keep her from finding time to spend with a man who really interested her. Just lately, she seemed to have lost interest in all the men she had dated, although she noticed that Cabel's social life was in full bloom. Terri had some formidable competition these days in the form of a tall, svelte brunette who arrived one Friday with a suitcase and didn't leave until Monday morning. She had followed Cabel's Mercedes down the driveway in her light blue Impala and Frances, in turn, had trailed along after them in her four-year-old Aspen.

"What?" She brought her attention back to her aunt's conversation with a start. "Sean? Oh, well, I'll meet him sooner or later. Yes, you, too, Aunt Helen. 'Bye now."

Gathering up the orange kitten in her lap, she settled down in the bentwood rocker and stared unseeingly at the watercolor that had been one of her first purchases of original art. Another man in the offing, and this one sounded no more fascinating than any of the others. Computers! What on earth had made Aunt Helen think they'd have anything in common?

Well, he'd turn up sooner or later, probably with a jar of homemade preserves. Her aunt usually sent preserves or pickles, while her mother always sent along something from the garden with any man between the ages of eighteen and forty who happened to be coming this way. Her sisters weren't so subtle. They simply handed out her phone number to the prospective victim and informed him that they had a sister who lived near Chapel Hill and would be delighted to show them around and give them a home cooked meal.

"Oh, horse feathers!" she sniffed, plunking the kitten back in the secretary drawer with the others. She had yet to determine the sex of her babies. Her own system had always depended solely on color: orange ones were male, gray ones female, and all others whatever the prospective taker wanted them to be. Meanwhile, judging from the sounds outside, Tripod had got herself stranded up a tree again. She went up like a shot but coming down with three legs was another matter.

Not bothering to drag the ladder from under the house, Frances located the frightened cat, treed by Cabel's Mollie, no doubt, and surveyed the layout of the branches. She grasped the lowest one tentatively and swung herself up, feeling above her for the next rung up among the lush cover of leaves.

Chapter Three

"Quit backing away, you silly cat," Frances grumbled. Her toe was on a branch that was none too steady as she stretched for the next handhold, and her fingers were actually touching the next branch when an angry voice below her erupted: "What the heck's going on up there?"

The words startled her and she felt her foot slip; then everything seemed to happen at once. Mollie yapped, Tripod leaped to the next tree, and Frances landed on the ground with a solid thud.

It seemed ages before the air began to fill her tortured lungs again and she blinked rapidly, trying to keep the black spots that danced before her eyes from merging into an enveloping darkness. She felt hands on her body and was too far out of things to do anything about it, even when they went over her with a thoroughness that would ordinarily have brought a sharp retort to her lips.

"Can you breathe all right?" Cabel growled at her. "Does it hurt anywhere in particular?" One of his hands was sliding down her leg and the other one was pressed against her rib cage just under her breast. She managed to gasp out that she'd feel a darned sight better if he'd get his damned paws off her!

"Temper still intact, I see," he came back, ignoring her suggestion. "Now, let's see if you can sit up."

"You sit up if you want to! I'm staying right here where I am!"

He lifted her carefully, feeling her back and the back of her head. "This hurt?" He pressed a lump on one side of her head and she caught her breath.

"Of course it hurts, you stupid idiot! What did you expect? Every single time I see you I end up getting battered and broken!"

He ignored her, his voice a deep, soothing rumble as he parted her hair gently over the rapidly swelling lump. "Skin's not broken, at least, but we'll watch it, anyway. Try standing up now and we'll check out your legs."

She pushed him away, frowning, as a solid weight of pain raced through her shoulder.

"You seem to have landed on your head and shoulder, but there's no telling what you struck on the way down. Anybody as clumsy as you are ought to have sense enough to stay on the ground. Even if you felt you had to go chasing that lopsided animal of yours, you should have used a ladder. An idiot would have known better than to go climbing up the way you did."

"An idiot would also know when he wasn't wanted! Why don't you leave me alone, Cabel McCloud? Haven't you done enough harm already?"

She thought she saw his eyebrows shoot up but she

couldn't be sure because his whole face was shimmering like a rainbow. Then he extended a finger and wiped a tear away from her cheek, studying it, and then looking at her as if he'd never seen her before.

"I'm not crying!" she declared tearfully.

"No, of course you aren't. Come on, now, up we go." He lifted her carefully, checking the position of her feet and running a hand down her thigh. "Anything hurt?" he asked mildly.

"Of course not! What could possibly hurt?"

"Good thing you had jeans on or you'd have scratched your hide on those branches. Although," he added judiciously, "you really shouldn't wear jeans in public. Not built for them. Some women are, but you're not."

She stopped in her tracks and glared up at him, too outraged to come up with words lethal enough to do justice to the occasion, but when he urged her along, she went helplessly because she suddenly didn't feel up to resisting any more. "I don't care what I look like," she lied under her breath. "I dress for convenience, not looks."

"Mmmm hmmm," was all he said as he lifted her in his arms and mounted the steps as if she weighed no more than one of her kittens. He went straight into her bedroom where he laid her carefully on the bed. By the time he straightened up and reached for her waistband, she had recovered her wits again.

"What do you think you're doing?" she demanded, pushing his hand away.

"Thought I'd check you out for any superficial ailments now that we've pretty well ruled out structural damage," he replied calmly.

"Check me out, the devil! If I need checking, I'll do it myself! Why don't you go on home? Isn't Terri waiting for you? Or maybe it's the brunette's turn today. She's got a lot more class, you know. I'd go with her, if I were you . . . quality's worth the extra cost in the end."

He grinned wickedly. "I'll have to bring her over for a closer inspection. One of her eyes might have just the slightest cast, I can't be sure. Maybe because whenever I get close enough to check it out, it's never her eyes I'm thinking about."

"God, you're dreadful! I only hope the poor creature doesn't wake up one of these days and find herself hog-tied to you."

"No chance of that. My policy of noninvolvement, remember? So far I've managed to enjoy the frosting without having to eat the cake and I see no reason to change," he replied with insufferable smugness.

"A steady diet of frosting can make you sick as a dog—I hope. Now, will you just clear out of my bedroom and leave me in peace?" Her head was beginning to throb by now and assorted aches and pains were making themselves felt, primarily in the area of her shoulder. She wriggled an arm experimentally, deciding maybe she'd better find out if she was going to need any help before he left.

"Trouble?" he asked quickly, his eyes narrowing as he caught her subtle movements.

"That's what I'm trying to find out," she grumbled, sitting up and lifting her arm cautiously. No bones broken, but all the same . . .

"Turn around," Cabel ordered, turning her before she could comply. His hand brushed her shirt lightly, then went to the buttons and began unfastening them very efficiently.

"Stop that!"

"Don't be any more of an idiot than nature made you. I'm not interested in your hidden charms . . . if any. I only want to see the extent of the damage back here. Your shoulder's bleeding all over your shirt." He completed his work and slipped the garment from her, taking special care with her injured shoulder.

Frances peered around, trying to see what had happened, but in spite of having an unusually swan-like neck, which her mother had always insisted was her best feature, she couldn't see over her shoulder.

"Hmmm, scraped rather badly, but I don't think it's anything I can't patch up. Where's your first-aid cabinet?"

Swallowing a feeling of queaziness as she saw her ruined shirt, Frances nodded to the bathroom and sat there looking helpless, ill at ease, and probably utterly ridiculous in her jeans and her lacy bra. But for all the attention he paid her figure, she might have been made of biscuit dough. Drat the man, anyway! She had seldom, if ever, met anyone who irritated her quite so thoroughly!

Returning a few minutes later, Cabel dropped the strap of her bra and then deftly unfastened it while Frances grabbed up her shirt and clutched it in front of her. She leaned forward, drawing up her knees and crossing her ankles for balance as he ministered to her with surprising gentleness. Fighting the urge to let herself go with the soothing spell of his hands, she said crossly, "I could have done it. You didn't need to bother."

"Show me just how you would have managed, then."

She slumped. Without even trying she realized that one of the few inaccessible places on her own body was her shoulder blade. "I could have got someone else to help me," she muttered ungraciously.

43

Cabel stepped back to survey his handiwork and Frances flexed her shoulder under its covering of gauze and adhesive tape. "It's a good thing you're such a liberated lady," he declared, "because you're going to have to do without this for several days."

Frances peered around to see him swinging her bra from one forefinger. She grabbed at it, almost losing the shirt that was the only thing that stood between her and toplessness in the process. "All right, *now* if you're quite finished, would you please get out of here and stop meddling in my affairs?"

Before he could reply one way or another to her rudeness, someone carolled from the front door, and Frances looked up with a stricken expression on her face to see her mother stroll into the bedroom.

For just a moment no one spoke. Then all three of them spoke at once. They backed off and tried again and this time her mother's shocked tones won out. "Fancey Ann! Why didn't you tell me?"

"Why didn't I tell you what? That I fell out of a tree and had to have my back plastered up?" Frances snapped, not caring for the gleam in her mother's eye at all.

"And your doctor . . . ?" Patsy Harris turned to Cabel, extending an eager hand, and both Frances and Cabel hurried to set her straight.

"I'm Frances's neighbor, Cabel McCloud. I just happened along about the time the accident took place, so of course I did what I could. No permanent damage, I assure you."

Meanwhile, at the sound of Cabel's urbane disclaimer of any responsibility, Frances almost choked as she made the introductions.

"Fancey's neighbor? Would that be the old Cairington place? My, it's a wonderful old house, isn't it? I know you and your wife . . ." She paused, looking hopefully at Cabel with her sandy-colored brows lifted questioningly above faded blue eyes, and Frances groaned, causing both of them to look at her curiously.

"No wife, Mrs. Harris. I bought it because I couldn't resist the view, but except for a housekeeper who comes to rake out the place three days a week, I'm alone."

Alone, my foot, Frances thought uncharitably. The bed doesn't even have time to cool off the way he shuffles them in and out of there!

"Oh, what a shame," Patsy Harris gushed in her best poor-little-me-great-big-you manner. "I mean, to rattle all alone in that huge old place. You must be terribly lonesome."

"Mama," Frances intoned warningly.

Patsy turned an innocent look on her second daughter and then, with a sudden switch of topic that was typical of her, added, "Fancey, I do wish you wouldn't wear those dreadful trousers. You just don't have the figure for them. All the Harris women are built on more womanly lines than these liberated bean poles you see running around town looking like ragamuffins."

Frances stifled a desire to giggle. Here she sat, mortally wounded for all her mother knew, without a stitch on above the waist, and her mother was concerned about the impression she was making on her neighbor in her blue jeans!

"There now, Mr. McCloud, don't you think Fancey has the loveliest throat you ever saw? So graceful . . . takes after my own mother, you know. She was a Sanford on her mother's side and they did say . . ."

"Mama!" Frances cried. Then, turning in dismay to see the carefully concealed amusement in Cabel's eyes, she grimaced at him. "There, you see? All my own teeth, too," she pointed out with an edge of rashness coloring her voice. Then, to her everlasting shame, she burst into tears. And while Cabel held her tenderly and eased her arms into her stiff, ruined shirt, Patsy Harris stood by wringing her hands and wondering aloud if she should summon a doctor.

"She'll be all right, Mrs. Harris." Cabel's authoritative voice cut through Patsy's soft ditherings like a hot knife through butter. "I was getting ready to take her up to my house for supper and you're welcome to join us if you'd care to."

For some obscure reason she was too spent to determine, Frances chose not to argue. She sniffed and brushed his hand away when he would have done her buttoning up for her. She heard her mother saying something about her television set being on the blink. "I'm going by Eli Whitney to see Milo and Kay . . . that's my youngest daughter, you know. I said I'd be in time for supper, so . . ."

Cabel saw her out and Frances tried not to listen as Patsy pumped him for additional information. There was nothing at all subtle about her methods, but Cabel chose to find her outrageous questions amusing. He also chose not to answer them, but he did it in such a charming way that no one could take offense. Well, it wasn't as if there were any big secret about her family's matchmaking propensities. Frances had probably mentioned it to Cabel before and if not, then he might have a clue now as to why she preferred to be independent.

He returned from seeing Patsy to her car and Frances hurried from the bedroom to keep him from joining her there. "Thanks for everything, Cabel, and I apologize for the . . . oh, you know."

"Any services rendered were probably owed. This

time I'll have to accept responsibility for startling you out of the tree."

"How about sharing it equally with me, then? I seem to have a terminal case of klutziness," she admitted wryly, adding to herself, at least where you're concerned. "Oh, and about the interrogation Mama put you through . . . don't feel singled out. It happens to all males who run across the female members of my family, I'm afraid. You handled it like a pro."

"Patsy's just a little more open about it than most women," he grinned. "I like her. Now, how about getting out of that gory shirt and then I'll feed you." He leaned against the secretary, now bare of kittens, and crossed his arms over the broad expanse of his chest, eyeing her analytically. "Wear a dress. Your hips are too broad for pants, especially as your waist is practically nonexistent," he said solemnly. "Fancey Ann, you'll never get yourself a man parading around here in those dreadful pants."

She bridled, then her mobile mouth twisted into a grin as she pretended to swing at him. But she drew back just short of connecting with that all too solid flesh. It wasn't fear of retribution, either, she decided as she slipped on a loose-fitting gauzy peasant gown of blacks, reds and golds. In spite of the momentary peace that existed between them, there was an underlying thread of something that didn't bear analysis. At least on her side there was, and she had an idea that any physical contact between them might just stretch that peace to the breaking point.

Back in the living room, she suffered his appraisal with ill-concealed impatience. "Anything else you'd like disguised? Should I pull a sack over my head, maybe?" After all, plenty of other men had seen her in pants and managed to keep their opinions to themselves; in fact a few even came up with a compliment. "Not all men are so narrow-minded as to think only women built like greyhounds should be allowed to wear jeans!"

"That rankled, didn't it?" he grinned. "I don't suppose anything I could say now would help, so I'll keep my opinions to myself, but allow me to tell you how nice your hair looks."

She shot him a suspicious glance. Considering that all women who could no longer call themselves girls should wear a hairstyle suitable to their maturity, Frances had worn hers up in several different styles for the past few years. Today, only because she was in a hurry, she had brushed the pinestraw out and removed the remaining hairpins and let it hang. Like a pale gold, silken cloud, she had hoped, although Cabel probably thought it looked more like a haystack.

They crossed the several hundred feet of sloping lawn that separated the two houses, and Frances was unable to keep herself from glancing at him as he swung along lithely beside her. No more tender solicitation now. She might have been a fishing buddy coming up from the river beside him for all the attention he paid her over the sometimes quite steep hillside. Unless she was torn and bleeding, he couldn't bother to extend a hand, she thought scornfully, angry with Cabel for ignoring her and with herself for caring. She supposed she was fortunate he was even thinking of feeding her.

"To what do I owe the honor?" she inquired disdainfully, mounting the broad, gracious steps to the verandah.

He treated her to a lift of one sardonic brow as he held open the huge, beveled glass door. "Mmmmm? You sound as if you'd rather not accept my hospitality. Don't feel obligated, Fancey. I don't mind eating alone in the least. Do it . . . oh, one or two nights a week," he admitted with suspect candor.

Nevertheless, he took her arm and ushered her into the spacious entrance hall. Frances swallowed her ragged pride rather than turn away. She wanted to eat with him. She wanted to see his home, and what's more, as much as she hated to admit it, she wanted to be with him, to spar with him in that particular way that seemed to make the nerves lift along her spine. But then, she had always enjoyed a good argument; her father had told her she should have gone in for a law career instead of majoring in art history.

The house was surprisingly attractive, although later she wondered why she should have been surprised. Filled with a compatible selection of modern and period furniture, with pleasing, unobtrusive colors, it hardly seemed the place for a single man living alone, especially not a man who had professed himself a confirmed bachelor. But then she too was enjoying her home and she certainly had no intention of marrying.

In one kitchen they ate country ham, potato salad, and homemade watermelon pickles that were blue-ribbon quality. "My housekeeper's a terrible woman but a wonderful cook," Cabel confided, tipping back his chair with a sigh of repletion.

"You don't exactly rough it here, do you?" she asked wryly.

His grin quickened. "Disappointed? Were you looking forward to a chance to show me your proper appreciation for all the help I've been to you, Fancey?"

"Don't call me that," she snapped irritably. "No, I'm not disappointed, and I certainly don't owe you any appreciation. After all, if you hadn't sneaked up and scared the daylights out of me, I wouldn't have fallen in the first place!"

"You, with what you yourself called a terminal case of klutziness? You'd have simply climbed higher and fallen even further if I hadn't showed up and saved you from your own foolishness," he jeered.

"I've had enough!" she cried, getting to her feet so suddenly that the table jarred.

"But Fancey, we haven't even had dessert yet," he taunted.

"You eat it! You could do with the sugar!"

"Worried about your hips?" he chided softly, provocatively.

"No, damn you, I like my hips just the way they are!"

Leaning over to make a slow, deliberate study, he nodded. "On second thought, I'm inclined to agree with you," he murmured judiciously.

Choking on her indignation, Frances stalked across the big, old-fashioned kitchen, and without seeming to have moved, Cabel was there before her, leaning indolently in the doorway so as to block her exit. "Oh, but you haven't had the grand tour yet."

"I'll buy the book!"

Her anger only seemed to amuse him, and that made her even angrier. She tucked her chin under as if considering a charge.

"Fancey, why do you suppose we can't be together five minutes without sparks flying. Have you given it any thought?" he asked as if he were seeking information about the best lawn food to try.

Nonplussed, she blinked at him. "Well, I suppose it's because we . . . we just don't like each other," she offered slowly, wondering as she said it if it were true.

Shifting away from the doorway, he studied her quizzically. "I wonder," he mused, running a well-kept hand through the thatch of his close-cropped hair. "Purely academic question, Fancey, but have you ever been in love?"

"Have I ever . . . well, not that it's any business of yours, but no, I haven't! At least," she tacked on hesitantly, "I thought I was once, but I've concluded that I'm not the type."

"Not the type?" His thick eyebrows climbed astonishingly.

She turned away, flustered, wondering how she had ever gotten herself into such a discussion. "Not the romantic type . . . the sort to believe in hearts and flowers forevermore. You ought to understand, for goodness sake, you said you felt the same way," she finished with an unaccountable breathlessness. The proportions of the large kitchen seemed to have shrunk, bringing Cabel uncomfortably close to her.

"But what if in spite of all your good intentions you found yourself interested in a man . . . that way?" he persisted smoothly.

"I'd put it down to pure biology and forget it," she retorted.

Cabel threw back his head and laughed unrestrainedly. Feeling at a disadvantage for some unfathomable reason, Frances tried to slip past him, but he was too quick for her. His hands came down on her shoulders quite suddenly, and only when she gasped and flinched away did he remove them, a stricken look on his face. "God, Frances, I forgot."

"I want to go home, Cabel," she managed weakly. It wasn't the pain in her shoulder that was making her want to run and hide, but the shattering feeling that she was dangling on strings and she couldn't even see the puppeteer.

"Frances . . ."

"*If* you please!"

"But I don't please, Fancey Ann." The mockery was back full force, wiping out any momentary softening. "Besides, your manners are lamentable. Didn't your mother ever tell you it was rude to eat and run? A woman your age . . . what is it, thirty? Thirty-five?"

"It's twenty-seven," she gasped, and he caught her mid-gasp. He caught her before she could do more than lift a hand in feeble protest, her hand trapped between the hardness of his chest and the softness of hers.

Cabel took full advantage of her awkward position to kiss her thoroughly, with a practiced sureness that left her other hand fluttering helplessly in the air. Her muffled protests grew weaker and weaker as his mastery took effect. And when the hand that was trapped found its way up to clutch his collar, he eased his hold enough for her to slide her other arm around his waist.

Even as he explored her mouth boldly, taking his time with evident pleasure, he was careful not to touch her wounded shoulder. Instead, with one arm holding her about the small of her back, he allowed his other hand to trail slowly up her side, giving her all the time in the world to lodge a complaint. Then he pulled his hand deliberately around so that it was lifting the small fullness of her breast, weighing the value of it in the palm of his hand.

She stiffened, sensing a mockery in the very playfulness of the gesture. He lifted his head to gaze down at her quizzically.

"Let me go," she whispered hoarsely, struggling to pull her scattered defenses together.

"I don't think I want to let you go," he murmured, nuzzling the sensitive nerve at the side of her neck.

She writhed against the sensations that the touch of his tongue sent coursing through her body. And his hand, the one that had held her waist against escape, dropped to her hips and splayed out to caress their roundness, pressing her hard against him with devastating frankness. "Stop that! You have your nerve!"

"I do, don't I?" he agreed easily as he caught the peak of her breast between thumb and forefinger.

Frances was stunningly aware of the effect he was having on her traitorous body and, what was worse, she knew he was just as aware. Her own body could no more disguise her reactions to him than his could to her.

"Once more, Fancey Ann," he whispered, his mouth hovering just above her swollen, throbbing lips to taunt her. But before he could taste their promise, they were interrupted by the sound of a car crunching up on the gravel driveway.

Frances's back was to the door, which put her at a disadvantage, especially as Cabel, instead of releasing her and going to greet his visitor, lowered his head to hers and proceeded to carry on with his ruthlessly masculine assault on her senses. The slam of the car door coincided with the entrance of his pointed tongue in her mouth. As footsteps mounted the steps and crossed the verandah, he slid his hands up her back slowly, deliberately caressing her until he inadvertantly touched the bandage he had placed on her shoulder.

She winced and ducked under the pain even as he lifted his head to stare down at her. "Oh, Lord, Frances, I'm sorry. I forgot about your battle scars."

"You didn't forget a damned thing," she accused stiffly, her voice low in his ear as she sensed the presence of someone just on the other side of the open door. "Let me go!"

"Well! Maybe I'd better go out and come in again," said a low, melodious drawl from behind her. "We did have a dinner date, didn't we, darling? I haven't mistaken the night?"

His hands slipped slowly, almost reluctantly, from Frances's arms and he said, "No, you didn't make a mistake, Olivia. Come on in, Frances was just leaving. Frances, this is Olivia Dawson. Olivia, Frances Harris, a neighbor of mine."

"A close neighbor, I see," insinuated the elegant brunette. It was the same one Frances had seen driving past several times and now, at close range, she was even more beautiful, the magnolialike perfection of her skin making Frances uncomfortably aware of the flushed sheen of her own face, just as the woman's small, coral-tinted lips mocked the nakedness of Frances's own more generous mouth. There was certainly nothing neighborly-looking in the crystal clear blue eyes that swept her with chilling dislike. Frances mumbled something and brushed past the two of them, not sparing a glance for Cabel. As her steps gathered an unladylike haste, she prayed she wouldn't trip over her own hurrying feet, for Lord knows, she couldn't see where she was going for the silly, stupid tears in her eyes!

Chapter Four

While the generous display of the crepe myrtles reached its peak and waned and the sourwoods rushed the season with a tinge of russet, Frances avoided any contact with Cabel. Her free half-days and her Sundays she spent visiting friends and family or canoeing downriver from Chicken Bridge, to stop off at her own house and provide dinner for the owner of the canoe.

The heating contractor sent a reminder that another payment for her expensive floor furnace was due, and after writing the hefty check she wondered how she was going to afford to operate the thing. Efficient it might be; free it was not!

But the wood stove that had come with the house still sat there, a constant reminder that previous residents had not had to range far to come up with a supply of heating material. And so the first free afternoon she had, Frances set forth, accompanied by both Tripod and Mollie, who seemed to have been drawn closer to some sort of an understanding by their mutual maternity.

Would that their owners could resolve their differences so easily, Frances thought, casting an unwilling glance at the pale yellow house she had fled a few weeks ago. Since then, they had greeted each other in passing and that was the extent of it. Which was not to say Frances hadn't watched that tall, lean figure emerge tiredly from the maroon sedan and climb the steps with a briefcase that seemed to grow thicker and heavier every day.

Armed now with a brand new handsaw, Frances located two likely prospects for her wood stove. One, a standing pine, was already dead, and the other was a hardwood tree of some sort that must have blown over during one of the summer storms. She surveyed the fallen tree doubtfully, wondering where to start. Somehow, back in the living room, thinking of a big pot of Brunswick stew simmering away on the cast-iron stove while the fall rains beat down on her tin roof, it had all seemed so plausible; but faced with the actual prospect—whacking up a full grown tree into serving-size pieces—was quite another matter.

It took her no more than thirty minutes to discover that a handsaw, and a cheap one, at that, wasn't equal to the job. She had tried her father's hatchet on some of the hardwood branches and watched it bounce back as if she were trying to cut marble. The standing pine was still standing, only now it had a blue-handled saw jammed in its resinous flesh. Frances plunked herself down on the hardwood and unbuttoned her shirt. The cool early autumn day had heated up rapidly once she began exerting herself. She had dressed for the task in a flannel shirt and her jeans, remembering with a sting of anger Cabel's acidulous remarks about her hips.

Of course her mother had said the same thing, but that hadn't bothered her nearly as much.

"Hell's bells, Mollie, what am I going to do, rent a beaver?" she demanded of the patient setter.

Mollie's attention, however, had switched to another direction, and following it, Frances was chagrined to see Cabel come striding through the woods like some silver-thatched Paul Bunyan.

Fine! Just what she needed—a witness to her failure!

"Mind telling me what's going on?" he asked mildly, surveying the scene with an expression in which Frances managed to read condescension, amusement, and mockery.

She cast him a sullen look from under her brows, taking in the worn white dress shirt and the equally worn jeans that clung to his muscular thighs with disconcerting faithfulness. The shirt, she noticed disdainfully, was open to reveal a thick pelt of chest hair that he must be trying to show off. Big macho deal!

"I'm cutting wood," she answered grudgingly.

He knelt and levered the saw from the pine with an easy, one-handed effort and then dropped down beside her. "Where'd you get it, a toy store?"

"A hardware store!"

"In the toy department. Was it deliberate? Is it part of the ploy to bungle the job so that some naive male will come along and say, move over, little girl, and let a man take a whack at it?" He tilted his head to cast her a skeptical look. Frances could have strangled him! The fact that she couldn't absolutely swear to the purity of her motives, knowing full well he had a chain saw and was adept at using it, had been pushed to the outer fringes of her consciousness; but she couldn't in all honesty tell him it hadn't occurred to her . . . which made her present position unbearable!

"If you'll give me my toy saw, Mr. McCloud, I'll finish the job later. If there's one thing I don't need, it's a know-it-all sidewalk superintendent who sits around flexing his muscles and making snide remarks while . . ."

"While you sit on a log and try to figure out how the hell to get the wood chopped."

She jumped to her feet and reached for the saw, but unless she cared to risk slicing a few fingers by grabbing the blade, she was helpless, for Cabel's strong, well-cared-for hand was wrapped firmly around the shiny blue handle.

"Just as a matter of interest, Fancey Ann . . ."

"Don't call me that!" she broke in.

"Just as a matter of interest, which was it you objected to most, the flexing of my muscles or the snide remarks? Or maybe it was the know-it-all bit. The male superiority thing that has your girlish nerves all atingle, hmmm?"

Mollie distracted their attention for a moment as she charged furiously at a pine cone, and when she gave it up and trotted off into the woods after livelier quarry, Frances turned to stare in front of her, a helplessness seeping into her bones that made her no match for Cabel's sarcasm.

"If you'll give me my saw, I'll see about having it sharpened," she said indifferently. She held out her hand and they both looked at it, seeing the contrast between the long, slender fingers and soft white palm with its angry red blisters, against his own hand, with its light covering of dark hair on the back and the strong, square-tipped fingers.

"You do that, Frances. Meanwhile, I'll bring my chain saw out and cut it into manageable sections for you. Do you want the dead pine, too? Some people don't like to burn pine on account of the resin."

"So what are you now, an expert on home heating?" she asked with a defensive sarcasm of her own.

"I'm an investment broker," he replied matter-of-factly, "but I have fireplaces, including those in the bedrooms, and I've picked up a few tips in anticipation . . . of the winter, that is," he added with an enigmatic glance at her flushed face.

"An investment broker!" But then, why not? She shouldn't be surprised that a man who wore custom-tailored suits as if he'd been born to them, and who drove a car that cost more than she made in a year . . . in *two* years! . . . should do more than dabble in this and that. For all the care and attention he had given her shoulder after the last time they had met in these woods, he might have been a doctor.

"How's the shoulder?" he asked with another of those disconcerting feats of mind reading he practiced too often for her comfort.

"Fine."

"You haven't fallen for anyone lately, then?" he cracked, and she glared up at him.

"Is that supposed to be humorous?" she demanded sweetly.

He lifted his lumberjack shoulders . . . developed, no doubt, from lugging a briefcase around . . . and she couldn't help but be aware of the scent of his clean sweat. "You fell for me the first few times we met. In the realtor's office, remember? Don't know which I found harder to forget, your natural grace or your ladylike vocabulary."

"Oh, thanks a heap! It took me all of two minutes

59

to forget the clumsy dolt who deliberately tried to trip me up!"

"If you'd given it another two minutes you might have remembered that I wasn't the one who lost my balance, or my temper, either," he said with maddening aplomb.

"Oh, shut up and give me my saw!"

As if she hadn't spoken, Cabel went on musingly. "You know, it's always been my experience that anyone who resorts to telling someone to shut up is admitting defeat, confessing that he . . . or she hasn't a single fact on his . . . or her side of the argument."

"I'm glad to see you realize we're arguing," she rejoined bitterly.

"When do we do anything else?"

"My saw . . . please?" she begged through clenched teeth. There was just no winning with this insufferable creature! He managed to twist her words so that she came out looking silly and childish, a hopeless case!

She extended her hand and he dropped the saw and caught her, pulling her to him so that she lost her balance and fell heavily against his side. Before she could right herself again, he was holding her with one arm, while with his other he stroked the tendrils of untidy hair from her overheated face.

"Calm down, girl, calm down," he soothed, as one might gentle a high-strung colt. "It's only words. You rise so beautifully, I can't help playing with you."

One strain of thought ran like a clear stream through her rocky emotions: she wasn't about to lose the last threads of her dignity by wrestling with him. If it pleased him to treat her like a child with a temper tantrum, why then she'd just humor him until he got tired of playacting and then she'd get up and walk away . . . without a word. Without a backward glance. She'd heat with gas instead of wood, if it bankrupted her, before she'd accept any help from him.

One stroking finger twisted a corkscrew curl. The warmth and humidity always made her hair react that way, and she was both warm and humid at the moment. He tucked it gently behind her ear and then began tracing the recesses of her ear, fingering the soft lobe caressingly. "Did anyone ever tell you you have lovely ears, Fancey Ann?" he mused. "You do; pink and white, small and flat, my kind of ear altogether."

"And you're a connoisseur, of course," she tried to sound sarcastic but it came out as breathless.

"Naturally. I'm an ear-eye-nose-and-throat specialist, actually, and I've already seen the quality of your eyes. They're unusually large, clear, direct, and in spite of all indications to the contrary, rather vulnerable sometimes."

She opened her mouth to argue and he closed it by the simple expedient of lifting her chin and holding it. "Now, your nose," he began, and she raised a defensive hand to that part of her anatomy. It wasn't a particularly delicate nose, neither classically refined nor pertly retroussé.

"Your nose is what I'd call proud," he declared sagely. "Not so small as to be insignificant. No woman worth looking at twice gets by with an insignificant nose; on the other hand, it can't be so large that it interferes with your kissing. Yours is just about right, I'd say, but then, only time will tell. Noses are cartilage, you know, and so every time you tell a lie, it goes on growing."

A burst of stifled mirth erupted, and Cabel gave

her a look of hurt indignation before going on to her next feature. "Your mother alerted me to the loveliness of your swanlike neck . . . although I'd already noticed. It was the third thing I noticed about you . . . maybe the fourth, but then, you have to remember, you were standing at the time and I was sitting down."

"Cabel, for Lord's sake, stop it!" Frances exploded weakly, surrendering to the helpless laughter that had replaced all her frustrated anger. How did he do it? How could the outrageous creature manage to disarm her every single time? "You make me feel like a heifer at a fatstock sale!"

"Hmm, well, if that were the case, I'd say timing was just as important as overall presentation."

She had to hear him out. With a dreadful sort of fascination, she heard him explain that if she went on the block right after a plumper offering, she might appear too weak, and if she went on immediately following an adolescent type, then of course, she'd lose in value because any prospective buyer would be forced to consider the number of years' service she was still good for. "All in all, I'd say that given proper presentation and an appreciative, carefully selected clientele, you'd go for close to top money. As an investment broker, I know what I'm talking about, so . . ."

Frances twisted out from under his arm, laughing as she stood and backed away from him. "You're impossible, do you know that?"

He nodded judiciously. "I've been called that . . . among other things."

"I can well imagine some of the other things," she came back witheringly.

"You did . . . at least I hope they were only imagination," he grinned, levering himself off the log in one easy motion. Frances wondered fleetingly what an investment broker did to keep himself in the peak of condition. Cabel was like a sleek jungle cat in its prime; capable of coming from a state of utter relaxation to full alert with nothing lost in the transition. She sighed unconsciously as she turned away to where the tin roof of her house showed through the branches of pine and poplar. The sun had already dropped out of sight and in spite of the echoing colors of its warmth, the air had taken on a briskness that presaged autumn.

"Come on, I'll make a deal with you," Cabel announced easily, a hand on the small of her back as he steered her through the clearing. Their footsteps were silent on the damp, pungent humus. "I'll saw wood while you cook us something hot and satisfying for dinner, all right? I'm in the mood for something besides Hazel's cold offering."

She slanted him a mocking look. "Aren't you afraid of being compromised?"

"We both know where we stand," he pointed out reasonably, "so I wouldn't expect you to trade on a momentary lapse. If we swap services, then we're even. The trees need cutting . . . beetles long gone from the pine, of course, but we need to keep an eye open for any more infestation, and the hardwood . . . it's elm, I'm sorry to say."

"So? That's not good?"

"Oh, it'll burn all right, at least it will after it dries out, but it won't split. Crazy grain. I'll have to saw it up into small chunks and then we'll stack it and let it dry."

There were three quarts of Brunswick stew left that her mother had put up last season and Frances tipped one of them into a copper-bottomed pot.

Brunswick stew went with wood chopping and, besides, she hadn't all that much to choose from. By the time Cabel came into the back door, wiping his hands on the seat of his jeans, the aroma of well-seasoned meats and vegetables filled the air.

Lest he think she was parading her domesticity out for him to admire, Frances told him quickly that her mother had canned the stew. The biscuits were her own, though, and Cabel accounted for seven of those before sitting back to enjoy one more cup of coffee.

"If the weather holds, we'll haul the wood to that flat spot beside your chimney next week, all right? Don't worry, you can do your share. I believe in full equality of the sexes, given equal tools." His grin mocked the quick lift of her chin and Frances relaxed again. "You're too quick off the mark, girl, much too quick," he teased.

She subsided. There was no denying that almost everything this man did or said abraded her nerves, but there was no point in carrying things to ridiculous extremes; and so, being of a basically open nature, she simply nodded. "I think it must be my conditioning. You know, the dolls and tea sets for girls, guns and cars for boys. Saxapahaw wasn't exactly the most progressive place to grow up in. Not that I'd trade it for anywhere else," she added hastily, "but all the same . . ." Her words trailed off as she lifted her shoulders expressively. "I just felt pushed into rebelling, somehow."

Surprisingly, Cabel volunteered the information that he had grown up in a town house in Chicago. "Went from town house to condominium to apartment, with damned little grass growing under my feet except for the few weeks I took off every year. Friend of mine had a place in upper Maine where the only females were moose and there wasn't a damned thing to hear or see except mosquitoes buzzing and fish jumping." He smiled an inward sort of smile that did strange things in the region of Frances's heart and she told herself it was the stew. "Did you ever see a grown man play at cowboys and Indians?"

"Is that anything like playing Paul Bunyan?" she asked innocently.

"Touché. Now you know I'd have chopped that wood if you and an army of liberated females tried to keep me from it." His smile broadened and he stood up, leading the way into her living room as if he were the host, she the guest. "Wouldn't we be more comfortable in here?"

"Unless you have a date," she said. "It's after nine, you know."

"Hmmm. Well, if I did, it's too late now," he answered, frustrating her curiosity. She snapped on the overhead light and Cabel immediately switched it off, turning on a smaller lamp instead as he murmured something about eyestrain. "This is nice," he gestured toward a small watercolor.

"I like it, too. I have another one by that artist in . . . " She broke off, her lips tightening as she thought of the connotation he'd put on the information that the other painting was in her bedroom. Come up and see my etchings! "And then there's the woodcut," she supplied hastily, pointing at a work that wasn't particularly outstanding but that had been given her by a bachelor friend of her youngest sister when he discovered she was interested in art. It filled a space and wasn't all that bad, really, but she preferred the immediacy of watercolor.

Cabel took the couch and Frances settled for the bentwood rocker, which had proved more decorative than comfortable in the long run. To her acute discomfort, now that they were seated in her small, but attractively decorated living room, conversation languished. Cabel smiled at her expectantly and she shifted on the caned bottom and racked her brain for a noncontroversial topic.

"D . . . do you think we'll have any more warm weather?" she assayed brightly when the silence became more than she could bear.

Cabel leaned back, stretched an arm out across the back of the chesterfield and laughed that deep, magnificent, unrestrained laughter that brought her to her feet angrily.

"Damn it, Cabel McCloud, you do it on purpose, don't you?" she charged. Untended since her foray into the woods, her once-neat hair had slipped its moorings, and now she blew upward at an irritating tendril.

His laughter dwindled into a few rich chuckles and he shook his head, his eyes sparkling wickedly up at her. "Oh, Lord, Fancey, if I do," he assured her, "it's because I can't help myself. You're so absolutely irresistable as a crusty little spinster, all full of bristly defenses, that I just can't help trying to poke a few holes in your armor."

"Damn you to hell and back, Cabel McCloud, you're the rudest creature I've ever met!" She pointed one trembling finger in the direction of her front door. "You're perfectly entitled to your own opinion of me, but you might have the . . . the kindness to keep it to yourself! Get out of my house!"

He rose from his seated position and she found herself all too close for comfort, but before she could back away he slid both his hands up her arms from elbow to shoulder and shook her gently. "Easy does it, girl. You'll blow a gasket."

"Out!" His nearness was having an unfortunate effect on her knees, and her mouth was suddenly dry. She moistened it with the tip of her tongue and prepared to level him with her second barrage when he swooped and caught her unprepared, covering her surprised mouth with his own. As a moan of pure hopeless rage escaped her, she felt herself begin to fall apart, the strength seeped from her limbs and any vestige of rational thought flew from her feeble brain as Cabel tangled an ungentle hand in her hair and held her captive to the depredations of his searching mouth. The heat of his hard body quickly permeated the thin fabric that separated them, forcing her dazed awareness of every muscle in the long length of him, and she moved imperceptibly closer, nearer to the flame that drew her to destruction. It was as if every atom of his masculinity were impressed on the soft vulnerability of her body and she wanted more, far more than she had ever wanted from any man before.

"God, you go to a man's head," Cabel murmured against the exquisite sensitivity of her throat. His tongue touched the pulse that fluttered there like an imprisoned bird, and she became aware that her hands were inside his shirt, her fingers digging into the taut flesh of his back.

"I think the rest of this evening's a foregone conclusion, hmm?" He began moving her into the bedroom, his arms holding her body so close that she could feel the play of muscles in his hard thighs as he walked her backward.

She grasped at a fragment of self-preservation. "What do you mean?" She knew what he meant! Her body knew, even while her mind was rejecting the casual thing Cabel had in mind. From making fun of her he thought he could go immediately to making love to her and it just wasn't on! Not by a long shot!

With some last resource of strength, she pulled herself away from him and clasped her arms across her chest, not flinching away from the question she saw in those passion-darkened eyes. "It won't wash, Cabel. I'm not another of your panting little playmates, who's willing to take any scrap of attention and be grateful for it."

Before she could look away from the hurtful intensity of those golden brown eyes, she saw the shutters come down. Oh, yes, he'd be backing off now, knowing he'd had a lucky escape! "Unless you've had a pretty drastic change of mind lately," she dared.

"Have you? Are you willing to admit you're not as independent as you thought?"

Armor securely in place now, Frances shook her head emphatically. "The day I need a man in my life will be a long time coming, Cabel McCloud, so you can just keep your fun and games for a more willing player! Now, will you please leave?"

"Oh, come on, Fancey Ann, where's your sense of humor? That happens to be one of the most delightful things about you, you know, the fact that we can swap a few bullets and a few kisses with no danger of entanglement to either one of us. Good Lord, if I wasn't convinced that you're a dyed-in-the-wool spinster with no hopes . . . I mean, no desire to find a man, that I wouldn't touch you with a barge pole." He was leaning back against the wall now, arms crossed, as were hers, and they eyed each other warily . . . at least it was wariness on her part. But for the life of her, she couldn't decipher the strange glitter in Cabel's eyes, and for some reason it made her nervous. She backed away another step.

"Why do you think I'd have dared to offer to cut your wood, or asked you to fix me a hot meal? Would I have allowed myself in your bedroom, even to patch up your shoulder, if I didn't know you were above any tricks? Come on, Fancey, we both need a cool, impersonal friend, someone we can relax around."

"I wouldn't call what you had in mind exactly impersonal," she reproached, trying for a slightly bored sophistication only to have the effect spoiled by a stupid blush.

"No problem. These things happen, honey, you're old enough to know that. Doesn't mean a thing, just old Mother Nature reminding us we're still alive and kicking," he replied easily, measuring her with a look she couldn't begin to understand.

Her head tilted doubtfully. She was vaguely relieved. Well, of *course* she was relieved, she snapped to herself, but then, why did it feel so much like disappointment? Why was it that all she could think of was what it might have been like to lie in those hard, muscular arms all night, giving herself up to the pure pleasure of the moment without a thought of tomorrow?

"Pax?" Cabel asked softly, interrupting her troublesome thoughts.

"Pax," she agreed reluctantly, watching him go with a swiftly fading smile.

Chapter Five

For the next week or so Frances and Cabel circled about each other warily, like two boxers sizing up the opponent's weaknesses. If there was an element of amusement in Cabel's attitude, France chose not to recognize it. For herself, she discovered she was spending far too much time thinking about her irritating, puzzling neighbor and she resolved to put her mind to other things. To other men, at least.

Doyle O'Hanlon, a man she had dated infrequently for a couple of years, moved from the periphery of her social life to front and center. She went dancing with him twice in one week and sat and listened to the Cowboy Band and drank beer, which she abhorred, at Cat's Cradle one rainy Saturday night.

On the next weekend he ordered her to wear her best bib and tucker for he was taking her to a new supper club that had opened up near Durham.

It would be a relief to go somewhere where she wouldn't be rubbing elbows with the college crowd, which got younger every year, and she decided on her coolest gown—a short, layered chiffon in shades of bronze, gold, and black—that hung from spaghetti straps to swirl loosely about her knees in handkerchief points. Her bronze slides had three-inch heels, which put her on an eye level with her date and she decided that that might not be a bad thing either. Doyle had been hinting rather strongly that it was about time for a few quiet evenings *à deux* in Frances's riverside cottage; and by the time the evening was less than an hour old, she was fairly certain she was reading the message in those light gray eyes accurately. Her spine stiffened accordingly.

The club was a converted old plantation-type house of doubtful vintage, but charming nevertheless. A surprisingly good dance band was on hand and music of the forties flowed nostalgically through the open French windows as they walked from the parking lot to the paved terrace where several couples were already dancing.

Opening into a large central ballroom were small secluded alcoves, with two or three tables in each, and the light was dimly romantic as Doyle ushered her after the maitre d'hôtel to their reserved table. The scent of roses and magnolias mingled freely with the fragrance of expensive perfume, fine tobacco, and freshly risen yeast rolls. Frances leaned back expansively and thought, this is more like it! This is the sort of place a man brings a girl friend, but how many men would bring a wife here once the honeymoon was over?

"Dance?" Doyle invited after they had ordered

from the over-sized menu. The selection was impressively small, there were no prices visible, and Frances felt the first tinge of dismay mar her pleasure. Oh, Lord, she hoped Doyle wasn't beginning on a last-ditch effort to lure her into his bed . . . or himself into hers. She was no stranger to the look-how-much-I-spent-on-you approach, which was one of the reasons she liked to pay her own way whenever she went out with a man, if she could do it without giving offense. On a date like this one, though, she had an idea that it wouldn't work.

They moved into the main room, with Frances following Doyle's intricate steps easily. She was a good dancer; she enjoyed it, but she wasn't really comfortable when her partner insisted on holding her as closely as Doyle was doing now, with his hand dropping below her waist in a suggestive manner that brought warmth to her face and a sparkle of irritation to her eyes.

"Mmm, that looks good," she murmured in an effort to distract him. He followed her glance to where a red-coated waiter carried a tray of baked country ham, candied yams and decorative curls of something green.

"I still haven't lived in the South long enough to take grits and greens with my candlelit dinners," he dismissed, nuzzling her neck.

"It's too warm for that, Doyle. Besides, I'm hungry," she insisted, backing away.

"Mmmm, so'm I."

Before she was called on to parry that remark, the music ended and she led the way thankfully back to their table. Romantic candlelight was a lot safer when they had the distance of the table between them.

While they were dancing, one of the tables in their alcove had been occupied and now the waiter was leading another couple to the third table. Frances looked around casually as she was being seated.

It was Cabel, and with him was Olivia, her black and white beauty set off almost too perfectly by a black lace dress that must have been crocheted onto her body, so well did it fit. Cabel smiled in a manner she preferred to call facetious and offered her the slightest bow, while his date lifted her nose another degree and turned her back.

During the next hour Frances was miserably aware of the pair behind her. They were seated so that her back was to Olivia's, which meant that Cabel could stare at the back of her head . . . as well as anything else he wanted to, and she couldn't do a thing about it.

Don't be an utter fool, Frances Ann Harris! Why on earth should the man stare at your scrawny neck when he has someone as lovely as Olivia Dawson seated across the table from him?

Olivia's seductive voice could be heard under the band, a continuous background, like the music of the Haw as it rushed over the rocks on its eager way to the sea. Only Olivia's voice wasn't all that welcome a sound. Frances found herself listening unconsciously for Cabel's deep, infrequent replies, and Doyle had to speak to her twice to gain her attention.

"What's wrong, sweetheart? I thought you'd love this place. I had to pawn the family jewels to hook a reservation."

She groaned inwardly. The opening shot of the battle had just been fired, she was afraid. "I know, Doyle, and I adore it, I really do. The food . . ." She had scarcely tasted the crisp-edged pink beef and the fresh spinach and the wild rice. "The food's superb and the band . . . I haven't heard a band like that since . . ."

"Since you were a girl back in the forties," he finished for her.

"Well, let's just say my parents collected records then and I wore them out when I was growing up, dancing sock-footed with Kay and Jean."

"Let's dance," Doyle said now restlessly. "Keep in mind, I'm not one of your sisters," he added meaningfully as he drew her to his side to pass between the tables. Cabel and Olivia stood just as they neared, and the four of them were forced to wait until the passing waiter had ducked agilely into their alcove to avoid a pair of dreamy dancers.

There was no help for it. Cabel was looking down at her expectantly, and she made the introductions while he beamingly extended a hand, as if Doyle were the very person he had been wanting to meet.

"Doyle O'Hanlon," Cabel repeated. "Would that have anything to do with O'Hanlon Electronics at Research Triangle Park?"

"Sorry. I'm with a small publishing firm. Sales end of it." He held onto Frances's elbow limply as he allowed his eyes the pleasure of Olivia's extremely low-cut dress.

"Interesting coincidence. Olivia's in sales, too," Cabel informed them. "You two would probably have a lot in common, O'Hanlon. I'll take Frances off your hands for a few minutes if you'd like to explore the area. No point in her having to stand here alone."

He practically railroaded the two of them onto the floor and Frances was livid! Really, of all the high-handed . . . ! She told him in an angry whisper just what she thought of his removing her date so peremptorily. He just grinned down at her.

"Come along then, if you had your heart set on dancing. I don't mind filling in for your lecherous Irishman."

"Doyle is not a lecherous Irishman and I don't care to dance with you, Cabel," Frances repeated repressively, holding back when he would have led her out into the swirl of dancers.

He gave her arm a jerk that caused her almost to fall against him, and then he wrapped her securely in both arms, disdaining the traditional manner of holding her waist and hand. After the first few seconds of allowing her arms to hang limply at her sides, Frances did the only possible thing and raised them to his shoulders. From there one of them, of its own volition, made its way to the back of his neck, and as the strains of "Moonlight Becomes You" drifted over the dimly lighted room, she closed her eyes and gave herself up to the pure pleasure of dancing with the man.

The hand on her waist dropped to her hip and she didn't protest. Through the sheer fabric of her gown, she was startlingly aware of Cabel's muscular thighs as they stroked against her softer ones to follow the dreamy strains of music. She inhaled in light, shallow little breaths, terribly conscious of the scent of him, the fragrance of clean linen, of tobacco and some elusive, exotic cologne, as well as a hint of male muskiness that seemed to grow more arresting as they danced.

Time hung suspended in the heat of the early autumn night and she was only aware that the music had ended when she felt the coolness of the night air strike her bare arms. "Cabel?" she questioned, looking doubtfully up into the shadowy face above hers. They were on one of the terraces, with potted palms and oleanders rustling in the light breeze, the same breeze that slithered her gown against her nylon panty hose, making her shiveringly aware of the raw state of her nerves.

"Our friends seemed so preoccupied I thought it only fair to give them more time to get acquainted. Who knows, I may have lighted a flame in two hearts tonight. How do you like me in the role of cupid?" he teased with a lazy, provocative grin.

"Olivia must be getting too close for comfort," Frances retorted witheringly, glad of an opportunity to put a little space between them. She needed to catch her breath after the exertion of dancing.

"Snap! From the looks of things, O'Hanlon thought he had a one-way ticket to heaven. Unless you mean business, Fancey, you ought to have better sense than to put yourself in such a position."

"I don't know what you mean," she prevaricated.

"You know exactly what I mean," he mocked lightly. "Three times last week and now the final knockout punch, the wining and dining and romantic music and a slow, leisurely drive home in the moonlight. Do you honestly expect to be able to palm him off at the front door with a quick good-night kiss?"

"Is that what you had in mind when you brought Olivia here?" she sniffed, moving away to lean against the stone baluster that overlooked a boxwood maze.

He followed her and dropped an arm across her shoulders, drawing her almost casually to his side. "I'm only a man, Fancey, and you'll have to admit, Olivia's a pretty fetching female. What do you think of her now? You only got a quick glimpse when the pair of you met." He looked down at her with an outrageous expression of innocent inquiry and Frances took a deep breath, determined not to be taunted into anything this time.

"She's beautiful. Certainly a darn sight better than the redhead," she added acerbically.

"Oh, that was . . . Gerri? Sherri?"

"Terri!"

"Right! Terri . . . uh . . . whatchamacallit! Well, I must admit, the wrappings were intriguing but the package was empty. Not so much as a tantalizing little rattle . . . just plain empty," he said dolefully.

"God, you're awful! No woman deserves such treatment!"

"They love it, Fancey. They eat it up and come back for more. Come on now, admit it, Fancey, don't you enjoy being pursued and then treated to a taste of caveman tactics? Doesn't it make you quiver inside with righteous indignation when the dastardly male animal proves all your pet theories for you?"

"Oh, shut up!"

"We covered that subject before. Do I take it you're surrendering? Crying Uncle?" He turned her deftly and she found herself once more gathered to that snowy front, her cheek against the sensuous midnight velvet of his lapel.

"I think I hate you, Cabel McCloud," she muttered, trying desperately not to let herself be stirred by all that blatant masculinity.

"Sure you do, Fancey Ann, sure you do. But then, we both know that a thoroughgoing liberated lady like you can take her pleasure where she finds it, just like we happy bachelors, without worrying about any deeper commitment, and it's just occurred to me that since we share that attitude, we may as well share the pleasure. Convenient, if nothing else, and if we find we're still indifferent to each other then there's nothing lost, hmmm?"

She opened her mouth to rage at him; the words were already on her tongue, but he captured her mouth, shattering her senses with an assault that left her clinging to him helplessly.

Oh, when would she learn? When would she know enough to turn and walk away instead of rising to his bait and leaving herself wide open for the hook?

Fragile chiffon proved no barrier at all to searching hands, and Cabel sought out the soft tenderness of her breasts, bringing them to a state of aching arousal.

"Cabel, stop it!" she gasped once when his mouth left hers to trail along her cheek to the vulnerable nerve just below her jaw. "This is a public place!" she whispered hoarsely.

"Middle-class inhibitions never bothered me, darling," he laughed against her ear with incredible effect. "Besides, what's so outrageous about a kiss in the moonlight? Do you think the management expects its patrons to settle for a rousing game of Parcheesi?"

One of his hands was stroking the curve of her hip, sliding the weightless fabric of her dress over the thin nylon underneath, and she captured it with her own hand only to find herself pressing his touch to her like a burning brand.

"You're a rosebud, Fancey mine, an autumn rosebud, and I want to make you bloom," he murmured against her mouth. His tongue traced the line between her lips. "Will you let me?"

With his hands on her hips and her breast, his tongue caressing her mouth languorously, Frances was all but demented. She struggled to salvage the last few remnants of her sanity before it was too late, and she found herself agreeing willingly to whatever Cabel suggested. "Olivia . . . Doyle! Th . . . they'll be searching for us," she cried, frantically backing away from him.

Cabel made a rude suggestion, using a word Frances wasn't aware of being in use among staid financial advisors; then he sighed and let his hands drop to the cool roughness of the baluster. "It might be better if we left them to find their way home together."

Steadying her breath, Frances grasped at conversation as a barrier between them. "I was right, then? Olivia's getting too close for comfort?"

He grinned at her with the insouciance of the unregenerate rake. "The trouble is, Olivia's a determined little girl. She insists on wanting permanent board to go with her bed and I'm beginning to wonder if the game's worth the candle. You, on the other hand, are no danger to me. We know where we stand from the outset, so what do you say we leave those two to their own devices and slip away to the hills of Haw?"

A streak of some nameless anticipation robbed her of breath for just a moment, to be replaced by a sense of loss. But before she could form a reply, they were interrupted as Doyle hailed them from the French doors. "Hey, you two, the band's gone into overtime and Livvie's gone and left me to powder her cute little nose. What say we join forces for the rest of the evening?"

Against Frances's every instinct, they remained together for the next hour, and Doyle divided his time between dancing with Cabel's date and his own, and even when he was dancing with Frances, he was talking about Olivia.

In a way it was a relief; at least she didn't have to keep moving his hands back where they belonged any more, but she found her eyes following Cabel and Olivia as they danced slowly on the other side of the room, with Cabel every bit as attentive to the exquisite brunette as if he hadn't spent those few moments alone with Frances on the terrace.

Had it all been some sort of a joke on his part? Was he teasing her, carrying their half-serious, half-jesting battle one step further? But the red-tipped fingers that now sifted through that silver-tipped hair were no joke, and Frances flinched at the shaft of pain that shot through her at the sight of Cabel's head thrown back in laughter. It occurred to her that her own head had been aching for some time, ever since Doyle had surprised them on the terrace.

On Monday Frances lost her job. Stunned, she leaned back in the corner of the office and listened while Howard Stinson tried to offer excuses.

Oh, there had been warnings—if she had had her wits about her instead of spending so darned much time thinking about her aggravating neighbor. It wasn't the recession; it wasn't just another small, underfinanced business going under. In the case of Orange Import, it was simply a matter of the small fish being swallowed up by the bigger fish. They had been bought up by a chain of import shops which had been cutting into their business deeper each year because of having a more advantageous buying position. But Frances mourned the fact that the cheaper, mass-produced merchandise would take over instead of the carefully selected, hand-crafted items she had taken such pride in handling.

"They're bringing in their own manager, my dear, because I'm too old to learn new tricks. I'll be the assistant, and . . . well, you see where that leaves you," he ended helplessly. "As it is, Myrtle will have to find a job to make ends meet. Of course, with all the kids in school, it won't be so bad, but good Lord, three sets of braces I'm paying for, and in a few years, three in college at one time. I'm telling you, Frances, it's almost more than a man my age can handle. Thank your lucky stars you're still young and unattached and can take your time looking around for something better."

Not so unattached, after all, Frances declined from telling him. She was very much attached to a mortgage and to utility bills and a heating contractor's expensive services. And besides that, she had developed a habit of eating three meals a day, a habit she hated to have to break.

Not that there was any need, but she worked out the week. It was as if the malaise they all felt flowed out the door and onto the sidewalk. The few customers who looked in merely glanced at the half-empty shelves and walked out again. Even on football Saturdays, with the town full of parents and visiting alumni, the sales were way down from last year.

On Saturday afternoon she cleared out her personal coffee mug, her small beveled mirror in the pewter-beaded frame, and her copy of *Diary Of An Edwardian Lady* and drove home an hour early. The heat had returned full blast for one last stand before Indian Summer gave way to hog-butchering weather. She opened her windows as she drove south on the Pittsboro Road, allowing the wind to have its way with her hair. Before leaving town she had picked up copies of the *Durham Herald,* the *Advocate* and even the little biweekly published in Bynum and now the wind whipped them about on her back seat.

There was no sign of a maroon Mercedes parked on the hill, thank goodness. At least she wouldn't have to put on a front to save her pride where Cabel was concerned, an almost impossible task at the best of times. She hadn't seen him since that night at the supper club and for that small blessing she offered heartfelt thanks. After a good deal of painful self-searching, she had decided after that night that the less she had to do with her all too charming neighbor, the better off she'd be. Something about him was decidedly bad for her self-imposed policy of noninvolvement, although she'd die before she'd ever let him know just how susceptible she was to his particular brand of charm.

Just a frustrated, inhibited, hormonal leftover, she chided herself in one of her more brutally frank moments. Maybe if I join a health club or go in for basketball, it'll pass.

The joblessness wasn't something that would pass, though, at least not without some hard looking on her part. The trouble with a college town was that there were too many lookers and not enough positions, and there was absolutely no industry in Orange County. Little enough anywhere within easy commuting distance from her home.

Her home. There was the rub. Ironic that her grand gesture of self-determination should prove to be the anchor, the albatross around her neck that kept her from going further afield in search of work. Commuting was too expensive, even with a moderate-sized car like hers, and she couldn't afford to trade it in on an even smaller one. Her savings account held enough for almost two mortgage payments plus the insurance, and almost enough left over to cover the taxes that would be coming due pretty soon. Her pantry revealed an awful lot of bare shelf, and Mama had already canned, frozen, and preserved everything in the garden and divided with Kay and Jean, who helped her with it all. Frances had not encouraged help of any sort in her stupid quest for independence, and now she was afraid she might regret her stiff-necked pride.

Pouring herself a tumbler full of inexpensive wine, she tucked the newspapers under her arm (after changing into a pair of white shorts and a rose-colored halter) and made her way down to the river. In the shade of a cluster of ragged field cedars she privately had designated as Daisy, Mort, and the kids, she settled herself, tucking her feet up under her knees, and proceeded to study the help-wanted columns. She had already decided that if she hadn't found anything by the middle of the week she'd go to one of the agencies that took an arm and a leg in return for pointing her to a job. So far, it looked as if she could choose between short order cook, night shift, and concessions at the Mobame Tobacco Market, none of which would pay her enough to live on.

Oh, blast! She took a deep draught of the wine and decided its quality wasn't up to deep draughts, only tentative sips, and then she took another one. A canoeist passed and saluted her with his paddle and then two more went by in close succession. She took another swallow of wine and tried to recall if it was an eight-percent or a twelve. In the heat of the somnolent September afternoon, it was acting more like twelve.

Draining the glass, she stood up impulsively and began to wade along the shallows, hopping from rock to rock for the most part and waving her arms wildly to regain her balance when one of them shifted under her feet.

"Fancey! Climb out of there, girl, before you

drown yourself!" someone called out after her when she had all but rounded the curve and was out of sight of her house. She looked over her shoulder and almost lost her balance again in the process.

Cabel was rolling up his pants' legs and coming after her, and she giggled and hopped to another group of rocks, out of the rush of the mainstream current. By the time she had gone another fifty feet, he was right on her heels, cursing occasionally when he missed his footing and ordering her to wait for him.

A minute more and he caught her arm, practically jerking her off her feet before she could wriggle away. "What the hell is wrong with you, anyway? I find a pint-sized jelly glass reeking of cheap wine and see you waltzing across the damned river like Little Liza with the full pack on her heels. Have you lost what feeble mind you had? Don't you know you could break your silly neck this way?"

It dawned on her slowly that he was truly angry and she peered up at him uncertainly. "Would you care?" she asked lugubriously.

"Good Lord, you're drunk!"

"Oh no, I'm not. I'm just . . . mellow," she finished demurely.

"Mellow, hell, you're loaded! Come on, I'm getting you out of here before you dunk us both!" He pulled on her arm; she resisted, and they glared at each other. "Look, Frances, be a good girl, will you? It's been a damned tough week and I'm not in the mood to go chasing a sodden naiad down the river Haw. Come on home and tell ol' uncle Cabe what's wrong, won't you?"

"Let's go down to Pokeberry Creek," she countered contrarily.

With a sigh of exasperation he asked, "Where the hell is Pokeberry Creek?"

"It's not far," she replied eagerly. "Come on, Cabe, I'll show you. Please?" She took his hand and they hopscotched along the edge of the bank until they came to a place where a shallow creek some ten feet wide led back into the woods. Frances tugged at his hand. "C'mon, the dogwoods are turning and the sun sets through them if we're in just the right place. Please, Cabel, it's just a little way."

They climbed out onto a mossy bank and sank down. Frances was glad to be still for awhile, for her head was misbehaving. Her fingers caressed the stiff fronds of a fiddlehead fern, and suddenly she felt terribly shy in the intense silence of the woods with Cabel's watchful eyes on her.

Somewhere nearby, a quail called softly and was answered as the small covey gathered together for the night. "Well?" Cabel prompted quietly into the hush of the forest.

She sighed heavily. "I lost my job. Today was my last day," she admitted, still not looking at him. The seat of her shorts was stained with moss and red mud and leaf mold, and her halter gave scant protection from the branches that reached out to snare the careless. Already she was beginning to itch as perspiration found its way into her small scratches.

"So?"

"So! What do you mean, so? I lost my job, I tell you! What am I expected to do now, starve? Lose my house? End up in debtor's prison?"

"I think that's been discontinued, but as a matter of fact, I expect you to go out and get yourself another job. Or are your talents so limited that you can't get another one?"

"Quit mocking me, McCloud! I feel awful enough without your taking cheap shots!"

"All right, for starters, exactly what do you do at that emporium of the exotic where you work . . . worked?"

"Worked is right," she echoed dolefully. "Past tense. I kept up with the stock, but lately Mr. Stinson wouldn't reorder, and so there wasn't all that much to keep up with. I kept up with the correspondence with some of our suppliers . . . that was mostly on the art-type stuff because I knew more about that than Mr. Stinson did. He thought it . . . oh, sort of added something to the atmosphere to have a BA in art history talking shop with the small galleries and individual studios, so he did mostly the wholesale warehouse end and left me to the individual accounts. And we had a bookkeeper to do that end of it." She scratched her arm and watched an ant crawl around toward her elbow before brushing him off, her eyes straying everywhere but at the man who lounged close enough so that if she had wanted to, she could have reached out and touched him.

After awhile she continued, since Cabel didn't seem inclined to break the silence. "I waited on customers and Mr. Stinson kept promising me I'd get to go on buying trips, but I never did."

"Surely there are other retail outfits who could use your services," he reasoned.

"Try and find one. I searched three papers today and there wasn't a single thing that would keep me in commuting gas, much less room and board. I can't go all that far afield, remember, because I'm not free to just pick up and move."

"So in spite of all that prattle about independence, you're caught in a trap of your own making, hmmm?

Possessed by your possessions." He leaned back, crossing his arms under his head, and gazed up at the arch of branches overhead. It was growing dim in the woods now, but the coolness was welcome after a day of near-ninety degrees.

"At least I'm not trapped by somebody who has me cleaning and cooking and sewing day and night," she said in exasperation.

"No? You mean you don't clean or cook or sew or do anything except have a good time?" The gleam in his lazy-lidded eyes glowed with disturbing fire in the shadowy greenness, and she stirred uneasily.

"Well, of course I do those things, but it's different."

"You mean, it's not work when its done for love," he prompted.

"I don't know what you're getting at," Frances came back suspiciously, "but I'm in no mood for jokes."

"Nor am I, Frances," he said mildly. "I just assumed you loved your little house and didn't begrudge anything you did in its behalf, that's all. I know that love for a man is totally out of the question, as far as you're concerned."

"How did we get off on this subject?" she wailed, rolling over on her stomach and cutting a rebellious look at his bland face. "I might have known you couldn't help me . . . Uncle Cabel," she added mockingly.

"Whoa there, girl, don't jump to any conclusions. Who said I couldn't help you? I'm just getting ready to offer you my special of the day." He lay there, long legs crossed at the ankle, arms beneath his head, and grinned up into the yellow leaves of a poplar tree.

"What's that?" Frances asked grudgingly when it appeared that he had forgotten all about her.

"What about all the other options? Sure you've exhausted them?"

Her shoulders moved, a small motion that made her halter fall away from her body so that a heavenly current of cool air seemed to circulate between her breasts. "There don't seem to be all that many, so you may as well make your offer," she said with a singular lack of interest. The wine had seeped away, leaving behind a growing depression.

"Marriage."

Chapter Six

Silence throbbed around her as the dampness of the mossy earth chilled her bones. "Marriage?" she repeated incredulously when she could get her breath again.

Cabel nodded, without bothering to turn his head to look her way.

"But . . . but what purpose would that serve?" Before he could answer, she sat up and shook her head. "I knew it was a twelve-percent wine instead of just an eight. She turned to stare directly into Cabel's suddenly opaque eyes. "Now, what's all this malarkey about marriage. Who? And to whom?"

"You, and to me," he replied laconically, turning over onto his side to face her, one elbow still sticking comically in the air.

"Stop joking, Cabel. I need your help, not your warped idea of a joke."

"And it almost kills you to have to ask for anything, doesn't it? In fact, you couldn't do it without stiffening your spine with a jelly glass full of cheap wine." He sat up in one fluid motion. "Look, Frances, it makes a lot of sense whether or not you realize it. Think about it, girl! What's the one impregnable position from which our independence can't be shot down? How's the best way to have your cake and eat it, too?"

Her eyes, the color of the small, mossy pools in the depths of the woods, widened. "How?"

"Simple! We go through a marriage ceremony . . . oh, all very legal and all that, but purely a business arrangement. Then, you go on with your life and I go on with mine. We can go out with as many people as we want to . . . Olivia, Doyle . . . whoever strikes our fancy, and the minute things start getting sticky, we flash our wedding rings and we're home safe!"

The fumes of the wine had mostly dissipated now; all the same, Frances couldn't quite reach the same exhalted plateau of sangfroid that Cabel had attained. "Are you sure?" was the best she could come up with. The logic of the solution somehow escaped her.

"Of course I'm sure! It's a natural! Here we are, two adults who have long since passed the age for any romantic foolishness. Well?" He looked at her expectantly. "Haven't we?"

"Oh, of course! Yes, certainly we have," Frances hurriedly assured him.

"Right. So as long as neither one of us is fool enough to fall in love, we've got it made. Then there's the property, too. You live in your house, maintain your own life-style and I live in mine, free to do to suit myself with no nagging, no one to have to account to for my time, and no role-playing. Cards on the table from the first."

"I . . . I think I'm beginning to see what you mean. But Cabe," she ventured uncertainly, unconsciously using the diminutive he had used earlier, "I still don't see how that gets me a job."

"Oh, didn't I explain the best part? Well, it works this way. I have a housekeeper three days a week. Dreadful woman! Drinks like a fish and I'm damned sure the silverware's walking out a spoon at a time. Also a few of my best pipes have turned up missing."

"I didn't know you smoked a pipe," she interrupted irrelevantly.

Cabel looked at her quizzically. "There's a lot you don't know about me. That's part of the beauty of the whole situation. No prying, no embarrassing intimacies. We could still be Mr. McCloud and Miss . . . well, make that Ms. Harris if you want to. How about it, would you like to keep your own name? No ego problem on my part." He looked pleased as pie for having come up with the idea but Frances shook her head in a small negative gesture, not knowing why, only knowing she was weakening to the whole idea and that if she took him up on it, she wanted to be Mrs. Cabel McCloud. In name only, of course, she added to herself in muddled confusion.

"No matter," he continued quickly. "The important thing is that you'll protect me from getting in over my head with irresistible females and if you need any help with overly amorous boyfriends, I'll be just a shout away, but back to Hazel . . ."

At her frown, he elaborated. "Housekeeper. Drinks, dips, and Lord knows what else. Got her from Olivia and that's the one thing that makes me keep her on. She's a good cook, though. And once I have someone to keep her in line, she'll work out all right. Livia swears by her. You'll get a regular salary for managing my household and when I'm entertaining . . . it'll be great to have some place to bring people for a change, restaurants just aren't the same. Anyway, you won't mind serving as hostess on those occasions, will you?"

"You could always find another housekeeper and Olivia would be more than glad to serve as your hostess," Frances objected doggedly.

With plausible earnestness, Cabel leaned forward, and she could see the fine lines radiating out from the corners of his eyes. His lashes, she noted to her distraction, were brush-thick and perfectly straight, with no hint of a curve, so that they could shutter his eyes as effectively as storm blinds, concealing any hint of expression. "But don't you see, Fancey, that's just what I'm trying to avoid. Lord, can you imagine what a conniving female would make of a chance like that? Give her an inch!"

"You didn't seem to think she was so conniving at the club."

His mouth twisted momentarily and then straightened again. "Honey, I'm no monk. I need a woman as much as any man, but when you allow a woman to insinuate herself into every aspect of your life, when you once let her think you have a weakness for her, then you're a goner. May as well just lay your head on the block and point your finger to the dotted line." He shook his head sorrowfully. "No, Fancey, as far as I'm concerned, a woman is made for enjoyment, and the minute she starts telling you what to do and when to do it, the fun's over."

In a small voice she asked him, "Aren't you afraid I might try to tell you?"

He looked at her askance. "You?" he snorted

disbelievingly. "With your commitment to independence and single-blessedness? The only thing that could possibly make you try to take over my life would be if you fell in love with me." Then, as if the idea just occurred to him, "You haven't, have you?"

Tipping back her head to reveal the fine line of her jaw, Frances choked off a laugh. The hateful color she should have outgrown ten years ago arose to add sparkle to her eyes above high, flushed cheeks and she blurted out her negative answer. "Good Lord, no! I was born with better judgment than that!"

"You don't have to hurt my feelings," he protested.

"Then don't go talking such arrant nonsense," she rejoined, getting to her feet to dust off the seat of her shorts.

Cabel gazed up the long, tanned length of her smooth leg and said, "It's a deal, then?"

"No."

He came to his feet beside her without bothering to use his hands, she noticed disdainfully. Show-off! "You mean you won't marry me?" he asked disbelievingly.

Through some trick of the deceptively dim light in the woods, it almost seemed for a moment that the muscles in his face tightened. Surely it was just the greenish gloom that seemed to rob him of his tan.

She was being fanciful. "Well, I'm flattered and all that," she declared facetiously. "After all, it isn't every day of the week a girl gets proposed to on Pokeberry Creek in broad daylight."

The wide shoulders lifted and fell. "Saved by the bell. I must admit, I admire you one hell of a lot, Fancey Ann Harris. Damned few women of my acquaintance would pass up a chance to take control of a five-bedroom house, not to mention a six-figure income, but then you're a class act. Not even to keep the wolves from the door will you knuckle under to expedience."

They waded out toward the golden light that filtered in from the opening on the river. "As a matter of interest, Cabe, why *did* you buy such a big place when you had no intention of . . . of populating all those bedrooms?"

He caught at her arm when she would have slipped on a mossy rock and released her immediately, even though she could have done with his support. "I didn't say I wasn't planning to populate them. I have no objection to overnight guests, although it doesn't usually take more than one bedroom . . . mine," he grinned. Then, as they turned to wade the river proper, his face sobered. "Matter of fact, I'm afraid I bought it on impulse. I came down here to North Carolina one day last February for a conference and it was sleeting like the very devil when I left O'Hare. Didn't think we'd get off the ground for awhile. Then I walked out of the airport here and you were having one of those spring preview days . . . looked like an Easter card. I liked the weather, I liked the people, and I liked the lay of the land. With no ties, I was free to move, and so I did. Nor have I regretted it."

"Didn't you have any family at all?" Frances was slogging along half a step behind him, the water chilling her feet now, and she saw the tightening of his jaw this time with no mistake.

"I have a mother. She's somewhere in Nassau with husband number four . . . or is it five?" He shrugged. "A stepmother in Madison, Ohio, and a stepsister living with her current lover in New York . . . current one being about the sixth in line, I believe. My father . . ." Here his voice changed, became noticeably warmer. "My father died two years ago. He was the first McCloud at McCloud, Inc. We worked together until he had his third and last heart attack."

She was silent while they climbed out onto the low bank, because she didn't know quite what to say to him. But then she saw that the familiar half-mocking expression was back on his face, and it was too late. She couldn't say she was sorry now, for the moment had passed, and so she mentioned the house again. "Well, I must say, you do your impulse-buying on a grander scale than I do. A pair of shoes or a double fudge sundae usually does it for me, but all those rooms! Do you suppose it will ever become known as the McCloud Place instead of the Cairington Place?"

"Who knows? One of these days it may belong to somebody else, if I get another impulse like I did that day in Combs's and Webster's office, the day you fell for me the first time."

"I didn't fall for you, Cabel, you tripped me!" Not even to herself would she admit the yawning emptiness that opened up inside her at the thought of no Cabel McCloud on the hill.

"Well, either way, no matter. Here, this place is slick," he murmured, helping her over a particularly mossy area. When he forgot to drop her hand, she didn't remind him.

By the time they reached her front porch the sun was well down, the air too chilly for her damp shorts and halter, and she shivered.

Immediately, Cabel threw a casual arm across her shoulders. "Sure you won't change your mind now, girl? Don't be embarrassed. I understand a gal's supposed to say no the first time she's asked . . . keeps her from seeming too eager. No, that's second servings, isn't it? Oh, well, maybe it applies to both."

She gurgled and her voice, when she told him he was ridiculous, reflected the fine tremor of her chill. When Cabel put the other arm around her and swung her easily up against the warmth of his body, she felt a return of the earlier wine-weakness in both her knees and her resolution, and she leaned her face against the earthy-smelling shirt he wore.

"Since I know we're both safe from any romantic nonsense with each other, how about a kiss to tide me over until I pick up my date tonight? I'm a man who needs a lot of demonstrative affection." Without waiting for her outraged reply, he lifted her chin and smiled warmly into her eyes even as his mouth came down on hers. She kept her lips clamped tightly together against his invasion and then, as she felt laughter shaking his whole frame, she jerked her head away in order to tell him just what she thought of him. He pounced, taking advantage of her momentary weakness to kiss her thoroughly and expertly until she was clinging helplessly to him.

His face lifted and his fine, clear eyes shone down on her as if lighted by some secret, inner amusement. "There now, you're not shivering any more, are you? Good deed for the day."

"Darn you, Cabel McCloud, I hate you!"

"What, for rising to your challenge? Or for trying to keep you from getting a chill?"

"I didn't challenge you and I was certainly in no danger of getting a chill. And you know it!"

One finger traced the line of her jaw, lifted proudly now on her long, graceful throat. "There's the challenge, love. Be careful how you lift that stubborn little chin of yours because one of these days, you're going to get what you're asking for."

He was gone before she could come up with an answer, striding up the hill as if he hadn't a care in the world, as if he hadn't proposed marriage and been rejected only a few minutes earlier. Well, of course, he hadn't a care! He hadn't wanted to marry her, anyway, and his job was secure. He could well afford to maintain a mansion for one man alone . . . or rather, one man and as many mistresses as he cared to install!

Oh, hell's bells! She let herself in, stomping heavily as she marched through the dark house to send a gush of hot water into the rust-stained bathtub. She had more important things to think about than any irritating man who had to keep on proving his macho appeal to every woman who crossed his path!

Doyle called to invite her to drive to Seagrove with him to see the pottery, and she declined with a thin excuse. He said, as if hoping to make her jealous, that he thought he'd ask Olivia. Frances replied sweetly that she hoped they both enjoyed it.

The next day, after a fruitless morning of job hunting, she got another call. "This is Sean Machlin. Your Aunt Helen's husband's nephew."

In a mood to plunge headlong into any activity that might keep her from thinking, she agreed to meet him at Crook's Corner instead of his driving all the way to Bynum, and they settled on a time. She dressed carefully, softening her usual hairstyle so that it haloed out to flatter her face. In consideration of the cooler evenings, and the fact that they'd probably be sitting on the terrace at Crook's, she wore a black midi-length skirt with a bold design in rust and gold and teamed it with an ivory silk blouse with a plunging neckline and flamboyant sleeves. A bit splashy, perhaps, but then, she felt rather like cutting a dash tonight with the unknown Sean Machlin.

Tilting her head at her reflection, she was reminded of Cabel's charge that she threw out a challenge every time she raised her chin; she ducked her head and tried looking demure instead, but it came off as a simper.

There was an exhibition opening at Morehead Planetarium, and they took it in between drinks and dinner. Sean wanted an introduction to a few of the local attractions, and Frances was determined to offer him a varied selection. For dinner they chose one of the newer restaurants along West Franklin Street. Frances found it exciting, for she was fascinated by different types of food, although she didn't think Sean really appreciated the plaki or the chickpea dip. He ordered Guinness Stout and when it came frosty cold, he drank it without demur and Frances, with the beginnings of disillusionment, wondered if he even knew better. Cabel would have sent it back quietly but firmly and asked for a bottle from supply, but then that was Cabel and this was Sean, and the two were as different as rocks and rainbows.

Oh, well, perhaps she was being unfair. Perhaps Sean was only trying to keep the peace. They went on to a party given by some people she knew fairly well and she wondered how he'd fare with them. In spite of all Aunt Helen's promising words, he was coming across as depressingly conventional, but she put on a broad smile and asked him if he liked homemade music, which was what the party was all about.

It was fortunate that he happened onto someone he knew there, for the two of them seemed far more interested in discussing football than in the music, which was mostly traditional folk with an occasional outburst of bluegrass. Frances circulated, nibbled the refreshments, some of them rather ambiguous, and sipped perhaps more of the spiced wine than she should, but she had a surprisingly good time, considering the fact that her date sat in a corner with another man and smiled at her from time to time as if he couldn't quite remember her name.

Sometime later Frances dropped Sean off at the house where he rented a room. He thanked her politely for showing him around town and she thanked him politely for her drinks and dinner. Rack up another frog, instead of the Prince Charming Aunt Helen had promised her. Not that she put any stock in her family's evaluation of men. It was a wonder her father, Uncle Jerrold, and her two brothers-in-law weren't total washouts, considering the Harris women's blind spots.

She had barely crossed the Chatham County line when her left front tire blew, with a noisy and frightening explosion that wobbled her over to the edge of the highway.

"Well, drat it all to pieces," she intoned exasperatedly. It was well after one in the morning and there wasn't a light anywhere to be seen, much less a phone booth where she could call for help. Her thoughts turned immediately to Cabel and she just as immediately rerouted them. He was probably curled up somewhere with Olivia about now, and the last thing he'd appreciate was being called out to change a tire by someone who had just turned down his marriage proposal.

Or by anyone else, she tacked on with all the fairness she could drum up. Damn! Face it, Frances, you've been staring at Sean Machlin and seeing

Cabel McCloud all night long. What if she had said yes? Would she be here in the middle of nowhere with a crippled car on her hands right now? Would *he* be somewhere wrapped around that sultry black-headed piranha?

She pried off the hubcap and then chased it into the weeds beside the highway, while she wondered if he had been serious or simply trying on another of his droll jests at her expense. Oh, drat, she had forgotten to take out the jack when she got the tire tool and the spare. Which came first, anyway, jacking it up or taking off the thingamabobs around the wheel, assuming she could get them loose?

For all her vaunted ability to look after herself, she had been singularly fortunate that the only other flat she had ever had was when one of her mother's lame ducks was with her. As a conversationalist, he was a washout, but when it came to changing a tire he was ranked among the best. She should have taken a few lessons while she had the chance, she thought wryly, wrinkling her nose at the smear of grease that streaked the back of her hand.

She tried to roll her sleeves up and ended up getting even more grease on her best ivory silk blouse. She let fly a few choice oaths of the milder variety as she wrestled with the machine-tightened lugnuts. A car passed by and kept on going and she swore again and then decided perhaps she didn't want any strangers stopping by to offer help anyway at . . . at . . . Good Lord, unless her watch was on the blink, it was close to two o'clock in the morning! The evening hadn't warranted the loss of sleep.

By the time she rolled up beside her house, she was dead tired, her finery wilted and showing lamentable signs of her recent struggle. Her hair was askew, thanks to a brush with a fender while she was trying to make the darned jack let go of her bumper. The chickpeas and spiced wine were having an argument with the barbecued spareribs.

Her hand had just closed around the doorknob when she heard someone leap up onto the porch behind her and she froze, her heart sinking into her shoes.

"This is a fine time to come cruising home," Cabel announced.

"What business is it of yours what time of night I choose to come home?" She fumbled with the key until he took it away from her and unlocked the door.

"I do feel a certain responsibility, although Lord knows why I should! Let's just say it's because I've met your mother and I know she'd be having a fit if she knew you were out doing God knows what until all hours, coming home looking like the tag end of a bad dream. Where's the boyfriend, or did you wear him out?"

She turned to face him, eyes blazing in an unnaturally pale face. "I don't know just what you think you're getting at, Cabel McCloud, but whatever it is, I don't care for your insinuations! You can just get out of here and don't come back! When I need your interference in my life, I'll send you a telegram!"

"You need more than my interference, you overaged brat! You need to be taken across somebody's knee and whaled good until you can't sit down! It's one thing to be independent; it's quite another to run wild all over the damned countryside until all hours without letting anyone know where you are! What if something had happened to you? Who'd have known, much less cared?"

"Don't tell me you'd have cared," she sneered,

struggling to hold back tears of pure, unadulterated rage.

"I should be so foolish! A man would want his head examined to care for any such headstrong, stubborn, reckless . . ."

"Don't flatter me too much, Mr. McCloud. It might go to my poor senile head," Frances managed in a voice that hardly shook at all.

With an expression of stifled rage, he grabbed her, practically pulling her off her feet as he hauled her unceremoniously into his arms. "If this is what you're looking for, you don't have to go chasing all over the countryside to find it," he growled, bearing down on her frightened mouth with an exasperation that bruised her lips.

Muffled protests escaped her as she twisted futilely, pounding his shoulders with grease-streaked fists. "Mmmm, damn you, Cabel McCl . . . !" she choked as he repositioned his mouth to plunder the depths of her aroused emotions. His tongue fought against hers and won, and she felt her anger seep away to be replaced by other, far less welcome sensations. Then she didn't think any more, she only felt as his hands gentled and coerced her body into a helpless, clinging mass of raw nerve endings, nerves that clamored for something that hovered just beyond the fringes of her knowledge.

The blouse was ruined anyway; the thought drifted idly through her mesmerized mind, like a small cloud on a sunny day, as she felt the buttons go. When her bra was lowered and the small fullness of her breast lay in his hand, ripe and aching to be taken, she moved against him, whimpering small, longing protests. Her hands were threaded through his hair, loving the velvety thickness of it, the live, virile feel of him as he positioned her against him. But when he turned her in the direction of her bedroom without easing the hold on her body, she dug in her heels.

"No, Cabel," she reproached, burying her face in his throat. "I don't . . ."

"Don't give me that, Frances. You want me as much as I want you and I can tell you right now, that's pretty damned badly," he groaned.

"No! That's not true," she lied, panic strengthening her so that she was able to pull herself free of his arms. She braced herself against the contempt she saw in his heavy-lidded eyes. "What's the matter, did Olivia disappoint you tonight?"

"Olivia never disappoints me, darling," he sneered, "but when I saw you turn up here alone, it occurred to me that you might have had a dull sort of evening, and it seemed the neighborly thing to do to try and cheer you up."

Just for a moment, she couldn't speak for the pain, but she wouldn't let him have the last word! "There's just no end to your good will for your fellow man, is there? No sacrifice too great!" She had to get him out of here before she either killed him or burst into tears.

He raked her with glittering eyes, taking in the further deterioration of her already disheveled state. She was miserably conscious of her tumbled mop of hair and the filthy, grease-stained blouse, now held together only by her dirty, trembling hands. She had never felt so much at a disadvantage before in her life and never had she hated a man as much as she hated Cabel McCloud this minute!

"Cabel, I truly hate you," she declared, her voice no more than a hoarse whisper. "I've never hated a man so much in my life and if you don't get out of my sight, I'm going to . . ."

He didn't wait to hear out her threat, which was perhaps a good thing. Instead, he turned on his heel and slammed out the front door into the silent darkness, leaving her to think of all the things she'd like to do to him.

Chapter Seven

News of Frances's unemployment could not be kept a secret for long, and she began receiving calls from members of her family. Her mother called first with plans to clear out Frances's old room so that she could move back to Saxapahaw. Then, when she finally accepted the fact that there was no chance of that, she promised to call all her friends who might be able to use the services of a nice girl who had graduated from the university with excellent grades.

At the moment, Frances might wish those good grades had been in a subject more marketable than art history, but hindsight was no help now.

Helen called next with the suggestion that she try the job market in Durham, put her house up for rent, and move into the spare bedroom now that her cousin Waldo was at Annapolis. "Oh, and by the way, how did you and Sean get along?"

Frances fielded all such suggestions with admirable tact and assured her aunt that Sean was a perfect gentleman. She continued to study the ads and pester the agencies but it was through Margaret Shober, the bookkeeper at Orange Imports, who had lost her job at the same time Frances had, that the first really promising lead came.

Armed only with the information that a salesroom for Oriental art objects was opening in the Chapel Hill-Carrboro area, and that they were looking for a manager as well as sales personnel experienced in the field, Frances set up an appointment with the interviewer for the following morning at nine.

A Mrs. Gwinn was meeting applicants at a local inn and as early as Frances was, she discovered there were three women waiting and one in with Mrs. Gwinn when she arrived. Hardly a promising state of affairs, in spite of her experience and the special interest she had taken in Oriental art as an art history major. She eyed the others and saw that they were doing the same to her. One was hardly more than a girl and could have had little, if any, experience but the other two were somewhere between forty and fifty, both smart-looking and confident, none of which made Frances feel very optimistic.

Her turn came next. She stated her experience, elaborated on the special emphasis that might tip the scales in her favor, and went on to relate anything she thought might be of interest.

For her part, Mrs. Gwinn was frank, friendly, and seemed favorably inclined. Frances's spirits began to lift. The salary was better than she had expected and, of course, the responsibilities were increased commensurately, which only whetted her appetite.

"There's just one thing, Miss Harris, and I'm afraid I'm going to have to be perfectly frank about this. The owner of the business prefers either married women or those past middle age," she said apologetically.

"But why?" Frances exclaimed. She had been almost certain the job was hers.

"It's embarrassing for me to have to say this, and I'd hate for it to get back to Mrs. Macheris, but the plain truth is, Mr. Macheris presents a problem. They both travel for the company, and as often as not, one of them will be here while the other one is on the West Coast or at the Kowloon headquarters in Hong Kong. Which means that the manager will be working closely with Mr. Macheris part of the time, and this is what Mrs. Macheris has to guard against. To put it bluntly, Miss Harris, he's a chaser and I wouldn't be fair to you if I let you think your qualifications were lacking in any way. They happen to be exactly what we're looking for but I'm afraid . . ." her voice trailed off expressively and Frances's heart plummeted.

To have come so close to the job of a lifetime! One that could conceivably take her across the Pacific . . . Good Lord, she had never been west of the Mississippi! "Would a . . . a fiancé do?" she asked hopefully.

The well-tended gray hair swayed as Mrs. Gwinn shook her head. "Sorry, dear. Engagements are a dime a dozen, but a real live, on-the-scene husband can be a deterrent that Mrs. Macheris might be willing to take into consideration. After all, it's not as if you were a plain girl."

"Well, I suppose," began Frances slowly, carefully, "I suppose we could sort of hurry along our plans. What if we were to get married within the month? Would that help?" She was out of her mind and she knew it. There was no way she could come up with a husband in a month's time, in spite of Cabel and his ridiculous ideas. All the same, if it would buy her time . . .

She left the inn with Mrs. Gwinn's encouraging words ringing in her ears. Better even than a husband of long standing was a brand new bridegroom. Not even the most suspicious of women could suspect a new bride of playing fast and loose with her husband . . . or anyone else's.

During the whole drive out to Bynum, Frances pulled the idea back and forth through her mind, examining every facet of it. Almost every facet, that is. She preferred not to dwell on her own preferences in the matter. The fact that it was necessary, if she were to secure this position, was enough to be going on with, and even that was asking almost too much of her after the way Cabel had behaved the last time she had seen him.

No. She simply couldn't do it. After his insults she had sworn off his company for good, and the idea of marching up to his house to ask him to reconsider marrying her was out of the question.

On the other hand, he had been the one to bring up the possibility. Why? Because he needed her, that's why. She hadn't for a single minute been fool enough to think he had any other motive, and certainly not just as a means of putting a little money in her pocket. That much he could do with a loan; not that she'd accept one from him.

By the time she crunched up on the gravel drive beside her house she had made up her mind. Now all she had to do was make up her nerve!

She changed out of her successful-career-woman suit into a gathered skirt of deep turquoise, matching it with a lighter shell top and a pair of multicolor print espadrilles, then quickly changed into her jeans and her oldest shirt. And then she stood in front of her mirror and muttered aloud, "Be darned if I will!"

That night Sean called and asked if he could come out and see her, and in a weak moment she told him he could. She spent the next day wondering why she had put herself in line for another night of boredom. They had very little in common. He was bored with art and she was not especially interested in computers. He wasn't interested in ethnic foods and music, and she couldn't abide beer and football. Besides that, he wore a bow tie!

Because she was thoroughly ashamed of her attitude, she put herself out to be entertaining, with the result that it was midnight when he left, in spite of her stifled yawns and her hints about an early morning. He stood on the porch talking while Frances wondered if she'd really sleep after he left. She hadn't been able to for several nights now, in spite of having nothing to keep her from it.

Contrary female, you're exactly what Cabel says you are: stubborn, cantankerous, and unreasonable. Over her thoughts ran Sean's monologue about fifty-yard-line seats and pregame rallies and she smiled sweetly as she wondered where Cabel was and what he was doing. In that state of absent-mindedness, she was caught off guard when Sean pulled her into his arms and proceeded to kiss her with an eager, slightly off-center enthusiasm that brought to mind painfully the last time she had been kissed.

Oh, hell's bells, she thought sourly as she closed the door thankfully behind him and watched the red taillight wobble away over her uneven driveway. No way would I deliberately put myself in line for any more of Cabel's mocking derision, she thought.

It was as if Sean Machlin had never been at her house that evening as she envisioned a dark, silver-riddled head of cropped hair, a blade of a nose beneath a pair of wicked eyes and a fatal combination of sensuous mouth and implacable jaw. Damn the man, why couldn't he stay up on the hill where he belonged instead of haunting her house down on the river?

The next morning, Frances poured over the help wanted ads once more and made a call to the agency—all to no avail. There was nothing, absolutely *nothing* that she could find to do that would support her and make the house payments possible, and she'd be darned if she was going to knuckle under before the third payment was even due! The thought of moving out again was inconceivable and so she dressed quickly and backed out the drive, swooping up into Cabel's section to make a K turn. Then she headed out for the highway, throwing up a trail of gravel behind her.

Forty-five minutes later she left the bank with a bankbook reading of twenty-three dollars and thirty-seven cents. The house payment was made and the last installment on the furnace was out of the way. She picked up a few items from Fowler's while she was in town and then headed for Bynum again. No point in hanging around town in case she weakened and bought something. The way she was feeling at the moment, she couldn't even afford a friendly smile.

A few minutes after lunch, which had been a bite of chicken for her, the rest of it for Tripod, and an

110

apple for Mollie, who didn't know any better, she got a call from Mrs. Gwinn saying the job was hers if she meant to go through with her wedding plans; otherwise, there was an older woman who had not the experience Frances had, but who had lived in the Far East for several years.

"I'll take it, Mrs. Gwinn," Frances announced without giving herself time to think. "We'll be getting married within the month."

Well, that settled it. Regardless of how distasteful it was, she was going to have to march up there and propose to that impossible man. Never had she thought to see the day when she'd be reduced to using a man as security, certainly not after all her fine prattling about equality and independence and standing on her own two feet. But there were some things she simply had not taken into consideration.

With her mind made up, she could hardly wait until he got home from work. To keep herself occupied, she baked a pie with the last of the apples her mother had sent her and then, in a spurt of nerves, she sat down and ate a quarter of it. She shook her wrist to be sure her watch was running properly and then took it off and strode out to the woods to bring back several armloads of kindling from the trees Cabel had cut for her. She had yet to build her first fire, and now that the weather called for heat of some sort—at least at night and in the early mornings—she found herself subject to all sorts of odd little worries about her chimney, the roof itself, and even the condition of the stove, which wasn't new by any means.

You *are* getting to be a clinging vine, Frances Harris! She dropped the load and went back for another. What if he didn't come home from work today? What if he had gone directly to pick up

Olivia? Maybe he even had another girl by now. Lord knows, he probably had a dozen! Safety in numbers, and he made no bones about liking women, which made it even more puzzling that he didn't just ask one of them to marry him. Ah, but there was the rub, she concluded, forgetting completely that he had done just that . . . if he married one, then he automatically did himself out of the others and he was a man who liked variety. He'd be easily bored by one woman, as witness the fate of poor Terri Whatchamacallit.

While she stood there with an armload of hickory branches, staring absently at a chipmunk hole under her woodpile, she heard the Mercedes drive up the hill. She dropped the wood and fled into the house.

Twenty minutes later, breathless, still slightly damp around the edges from her quick shower, Frances strolled with feigned unconcern up the grassy slope to the yellow house. She rapped on the door before she lost her nerve, and when no one answered immediately, she turned and was halfway down the steps when the door opened behind her.

Framed in the doorway was the tall figure of Cabel McCloud, his ice-blue shirttail hanging out of the creased trousers of his summer suit and even as she watched, he unfastened the last button and tugged the already loosened tie from his neck. "Want me?" he asked easily.

With her eyes focused somewhere below the base of his throat, Frances opened her mouth to speak, cleared her throat, and made another effort. "Could . . . would it be possible to see you?"

"Any particular part, or just my chest?" he taunted, and her eyes flew up to reproach him as wild color stained her cheeks.

"Come on inside, Frances." He stepped back and

held the door for her and she had to force her feet to obey her mind, for it was almost more than she could do, to squeeze past him and enter his foyer.

He knew it, too, and he wasn't going to make it any easier for her. It was almost as if he knew her purpose in coming and was determined to draw the last bit of satisfaction from her embarrassment. Leading her into the gracious living room, he said, "You haven't seen my house, have you?"

"Yes, I have. You've forgotten."

He lifted a shoulder nonchalantly and continued to remove his thin gold watch, laying it carelessly on the mantel before turning to her expectantly. "Did you just drop in for a neighborly chat or had you something more specific in mind?"

"No. I mean yes. I mean . . ." Oh, Lord, how did one go about rescinding a rejection? She closed her eyes momentarily and breathed deeply while he waited with a pleasant, impersonal little smile on his face. "Look, Cabel, did you mean what you said the other day?"

"Which was that?"

"Oh, you know! About . . . about needing a housekeeper and a hostess."

"Oh, yes . . . my offer of employment. Well, I don't suppose it could be called employment in the strictest sense . . . maybe a supervisory capacity, but . . ."

"Damn it, Cabel, stop that! Either you will or you won't, and at the moment, I don't really care much which one, but don't play your childish little games with me! Just tell me yes or no!"

"I'd be delighted to oblige, Fancey, if I had any idea of what it was you were asking," he declared with mild exasperation.

Her fists balled in the pocket of her skirt and

unconsciously she lifted her chin another two degrees. "Marry me."

Without looking directly at him, Frances had an impression of sudden stillness, and then he shifted so that his feet were braced apart, the powerful muscles of his thighs clearly evident under the lightweight stuff of his trousers. He extended an arm casually along the mantle and leveled his gaze at her. "All right."

She expelled the breath she wasn't even conscious of having held as her eyes flew to his face. "All right?" she repeated dazedly.

He nodded. "Sure. If that's what you want, I don't mind obliging you. As I mentioned the first time we discussed the matter, it will be convenient for me not to have to worry about the ordering of my household."

Oh, how romantic we are, she thought, biting her bottom lip against a sudden hysterical desire to laugh. "Fine, then," she gulped. "When?"

He glanced at his watch, as if expecting her to try and drag him off to a registrar's office before it closed for the day, and she tried for an offhand note when she replied that it didn't matter all that much: "It's only that there's this job," she explained.

"I didn't think it was my fatal charm," Cabel retorted dryly.

She went on as if she hadn't heard him. "I have the right qualifications and it's a marvelous position, only the husband . . . well, he chases, according to the woman who interviewed me for the owners. No single ladies under forty need apply, or words to that effect." She watched him closely, anxiously willing him to understand that there was absolutely nothing personal in it at all. "I told her within the month," she added timidly.

A square-tipped hand lifted to stroke the stubble on his chin and Frances watched the rhythmic movements with growing fascination. There was a flat, matted place on his hirsute wrist where his watch had been, and for some queer reason, it was all she could do not to reach out and touch it. Her fingernails bit into her palm as she waited for him to speak.

"One day next week will be soon enough, then? I'm afraid it's the best I can do. I'm taking Olivia to Roaring Gap for the weekend, and on Monday I'll probably be pretty well worn out . . . Tuesday, then. Shall we get started on the preliminaries on Tuesday?" He looked at her blandly, as if he were mentally shuffling through his engagement book, and she felt about three feet tall.

"Fine," she said through gritted teeth.

One hand tucked under his low-riding belt, Cabel lifted the other to stroke the back of his neck as he stifled a yawn. "Damn, I'm tired. Didn't get in until almost one last night, then up at the crack of dawn. Getting too old for that sort of foolishness." He looked at her with a disarming grin. "Maybe it'll settle me down, this business of marriage."

She resented the flash of white teeth, resented the handsome face, and resented being put in the position of an object of charity. "All right, then, Tuesday," she said grudgingly.

"Great. Call my secretary first thing and she'll tell you what time . . . No, on second thought, why don't we make it twelve-thirty. I can take time out to give you lunch and then we can sort out the red tape on the way back to the office. When do you start?"

"Start?" she echoed stupidly.

"Work. The new job."

"Oh. Next week, I guess. I forgot to ask."

He looked at her curiously and picked up his watch from the mantle. "Was there anything else?" he asked politely.

Flushing, she jumped to her feet. On her hasty way to the door his voice followed her, "It's only that I have a dinner date and as we're driving to Raleigh, I can't afford to be too late in starting off."

"Oh . . . !" She made her escape noisily, slamming the door behind her in an excess of childish bad manners. If only she could have thought of something devastatingly cutting to say to him, but he robbed her of even that satisfaction, his very calmness pushing her to the upper limits of rage. The man was absolutely the most infuriating, enraging, insufferable . . . !

The list carried her halfway down the hill and she decided adamantly that she wouldn't marry him if she were to be burned at the stake!

They were married in the office of a justice of the peace; oddly enough, it had been Cabel who had tried to talk her into having a church wedding with friends and family in attendance. All the time she was spouting her piece about business arrangements and the importance of maintaining an impersonal atmosphere, something inside her was drifting closer and closer to the surface of her consciousness. And because her every instinct of self-preservation forced her to ignore it, she insisted on the minimum of fuss.

Which was not to say that she didn't wear a dress of uncharacteristic frailty, an ivory georgette street-length dress whose effectiveness was due to the fineness of fabric and cut instead of any frills. And when Cabel handed her a nosegay of Talisman rosebuds, it was all she could do to maintain her composure. With her chin tilted to an imperious degree, she accepted the tearful best wishes of her family and practically dragged Cabel from the waiting room, where everyone stood around talking about other weddings and happy brides and all the things she least wanted to think about.

They left the building with Cabel's fingers biting into her arm, and his increasingly grim countenance hovered somewhere between her nervous glance and the steady stream of downtown traffic. She waited impatiently for two cyclists to pass and then stepped off the curb in front of a van, only to be jerked back by Cabel's far from gentle strength.

"Damn it to hell, Frances, don't make me a widower before I'm even a bridegroom!" he snarled.

She stood trembling on the edge of the sidewalk, oblivious to passersby, and he stared down into her bleached face with a baffled sort of anger. Then, as if defeated by something he saw there, he propelled her to where his car waited.

By the time they had left the fringes of Chapel Hill, she was able to breathe more freely and the feeling of faintness had left her. What on earth was the matter with her? She usually managed to dodge in and out of traffic with all the ease of a practiced jaywalker, so why now, with only the normal Friday afternoon traffic, did she seem bent on self-destruction?

"Feeling better?" he asked curtly, tilting a vent to deflect a stream of air into her face.

"I guess I ought to thank you," she conceded.

"Don't overdo it."

She twisted in her seat, conscious of the buttery soft leather beneath her lightweight coat. "I'm sorry, Cabel. I don't know what's wrong with me. I'm not usually so dense, believe it or not."

He slanted her a closed sort of look as he directed the heavy car with the same skill he brought to everything he did. "Traditional wedding jitters?" he asked laconically.

"That's hardly applicable in this case, is it?"

Beneath the custom fit of his medium gray suit, a shoulder moved disparagingly. "You tell me," he invited in an offhand voice.

She bit her lip. "Well, after all, it's not as if we were really married," she began, when he interrupted her to demand softly just what she thought the ceremony meant.

"Oh . . . it means . . . it means you can use me as an excuse whenever one of your girl friends gets a little too demanding," she said with commendable lightness. "I understand from a tax standpoint we'll both suffer, but maybe I can save you enough on your housekeeping bills to make up the difference."

The car veered suddenly into the muddy entrance of a sloping pasture, and with numbed anticipation, Frances watched as a dozen or so Herefords lifted white faces to stare benignly at them. "Listen here to me, Fancey, you're my wife!" Cabel ground out, "With all the rights and privileges that term entails, and if . . ."

"No!"

"What do you mean, no?" A dangerously silky note had entered Cabel's deep voice.

"I mean . . . no rights, no privileges. You know that, Cabel," she pleaded, suddenly abandoning her spurious defenses. "Look, we both agreed that we wanted to stay . . . well, unattached, unentangled, and have all the . . . the benefits of marriage with none of the hazards."

"Perhaps you'd care to enlighten me on which is which?" he asked mildly. Somewhere along the line he had picked up her wrist and now his thumb was playing games with the sensitive skin over her throbbing pulse.

"I . . . I'll take charge of Hazel for you, and hostess any business dinners and you . . ." Her eyes flew up to meet his mocking glance and it was as if his eyes were challenging her, provoking her into what, she couldn't say. She rushed into speech, "And you'll be perfectly free to . . . to carry on as usual. I . . . I won't ask anything of you but the use of your name." Her glance dropped to her third finger, left hand, where, to her continued amazement, a hand-wrought gold and jade ring nestled beside the plain wedding band.

"That's big of you, Fancey Ann McCloud," he allowed softly, turning her hand in his and bringing it up to his lips.

While she hung there, suspended by the burning power of his eyes, he deliberately touched the center of her palm with the tip of his tongue, caressing a nerve that seemed to have a direct line to the center of her body. Her head fell back slightly as her eyelids drooped and she whispered unsteadily, "Cabel, don't do that."

"Do what?"

"You know very well what. We're . . . we're both experienced adults and we both know very well where this sort of thing can lead." Her voice could have been drifting in through the open window like the sound of cicadas on the earthy-sweet pungence of the pasture, so ephemeral was it. She hoped to God he hadn't any real idea just how limited her own experience was. He could wipe her out, totally annihilate her without half trying if she allowed it to happen, and then walk away without a backward glance.

Abruptly, he started the car. He didn't speak the rest of the way home and when, instead of dropping her off at her own house he continued on up the hill, she didn't protest.

"I thought you might want to familiarize yourself with the house, since Hazel comes tomorrow. The bedrooms and baths upstairs, linen closets, storerooms, and all the places you women like to spend endless hours talking about," Cabel mentioned, ushering her inside and closing the door against the increasing coolness as the sun settled down behind the wooded hills.

"You've a flattering opinion of my conversation, haven't you?"

"Nothing personal, Frances. Just thought you ought to check the place out if you've nothing else planned for the next few minutes." He was tugging loose his crisp silk tie and unbuttoning the neck of his shirt as he spoke, and he took the stairs two at a time, calling over his shoulder, "I'll be in the first room on the right if you need me for anything."

She was on the bottom step when Cabel reached the top and he turned to stare down at her, his foreshortened body looking even more threateningly masculine from her vantage point below him. She stood poised there, one slender foot in a bone calf T-strap resting uncertainly on the second step as she raised her face to him. In a split-second vision, one of those subliminal flashes that sometimes occur, she saw herself dressed in the mode of a previous century, looking up those same graceful stairs to where her husband stood, legs braced apart in frock coat, waistcoat, and dark, fitted pantaloons, his virile physique a magnet for her eyes as she asked in a strained voice, *Will you be long?*

"Will you be long?" she asked now, in the same

120

strained tone. She blinked to dispell the disturbing effect of déjà vu, never losing contact with those curiously shuttered brown eyes.

"You mean now? I'm only going to change clothes, why?"

"Oh, no reason." She dropped back to the polished floor, still more shaken than she cared to reveal. "I just wondered. I . . . I'll look around downstairs first and then I think I'd better run along home. Tripod needs feeding. She's been neglected since I gave away her babies."

He nodded and shrugged out of his shirt, his hand going to his belt buckle. "Right. Well, I probably won't see you again before I leave, then, so how about locking up for me if you're still here when I go. I'll be late getting home, I expect."

She took it like a stiff blow to the solar plexus, only glad he had already turned away. He was saying goodnight to her! He had no plans to spend so much as an unnecessary minute with her on their own wedding night! She winced as she turned to hurry away to the back of the house, her eyes burning as she stared unseeingly at the bank of wooden-buttoned cabinets that lined the hallway leading to the large, old-fashioned kitchen.

Blast! Oh, just blast the hateful creature to smithereens! She heard the sound of his footsteps overhead, brisk, sure and firm; and when they clattered downstairs, she hurried over and yanked open one of the cabinet doors, staring intently at the rows of canned goods and unmarked cannisters when she felt his presence behind her.

With every cell in her body alert while she stood rigidly in position, she was still unprepared when his hand descended to her shoulder.

"I think on today, at least, I might claim this

much," he said, giving her no chance to protest as his mouth came down on hers.

She resisted, her mouth clamped tightly shut as he teased the line between her lips with the tip of his tongue. His hands curled over her shoulders to tuck into the intimate warmth under her arms and he brushed his lips softly over hers, taunting her, making fun of her adamancy until she could have cried out in wretched frustration. There was no hiding her trembling from him, and his arms slipped across her back to draw her more closely to him, still without force, still without more than the most teasing hint of passion. But it was too much for her unsheathed nerves, and she ducked her face into the soft collar of his black knit shirt, burrowing into the clean scented firm flesh of his throat.

Neither of them spoke, nor did they move for unreckoned moments, and then, slowly, she became aware that Cabel's palm was smoothing the thin fabric of her skirt over her hips and tucking under the roundedness to bring her into closer proximity to his own stirring body. Against his throat, her lips opened and her tongue dared taste the faint sweet-saltiness of his flesh. Then he came fully alive, the length of his whole frame registering arousal as he lifted her chin and sought her eager mouth with his.

The kitchen. Why was it they always seemed to make love in the kitchen, she wondered fleetingly, and then all rational thought was swept from her mind as Cabel lifted her in his arms and strode through to the living room, to lower her onto one of the two long, quilted, feather-cushioned sofas. He positioned himself beside her, making her a prisoner with his body, and then he grinned down into her face, his eyes looking almost black as the pupils reflected her flushed, touseled appearance just before he kissed her again.

Buttons magically found themselves unbuttoned, her side zipper was released, and her skirt had somehow crept up over the satin of her slip. She laughed and whispered shakily, "I thought you were going out."

"I lied," he replied with engaging smugness as he released the catch of her lacy wisp of bra and then frowned comically down at the confusion of straps and sleeves about her shoulders. "Hmmm . . . there's got to be a better way to handle this."

"And you're the big lady's man," she chided audaciously.

"Ah, but you're no lady; you're my wife," he shot back triumphantly as he succeeded in baring her to the waist. His face went quite still as his eyes played over her body. "Oh, Lord, you're so very lovely, Frances," he breathed feelingly, and then he bent to capture the shy-proud peak of her breast between his lips, caressing it with his tongue until her head was writhing helplessly against the pillow.

"I can't take much more of this, love," he managed in a voice completely unlike his usual assured tones. "Let's go to bed before you push me quietly over the edge of sanity." He got up and took a deep breath. "I'll lock up, darling, because we may not be downstairs before Monday morning," he warned, extending a hand to help her to her feet.

"You look enchanting, Mrs. McCloud, with your hair falling all over your naked shoulders, but your untidy dress . . . tsk, tsk, tsk!" He shook his head with playful sternness as he allowed his hands the freedom of her body, covering her breasts, and then trailing a finger down to where her narrow gold belt still held the drapery of satin and georgette gathered about her hips. "Shocking, darling . . . positively indecent! Wait for me, hmmm?"

He turned and strode away and Frances stared after him with bemused eyes. Was this the man she had married? This tender, mocking playmate whom she could affect so marvelously with her body? Perhaps there was a chance for their union, after all. Even as hope arose like a newly sprouted seed just breaking through the earth's darkness to see the light of the sun, the phone beside her rang and, still in a state of euphoria, she lifted it unconsciously and spoke.

"Let me speak to Cabel! Who is this, anyway?"

Blighted hope withered away and turned inward again. "This is Frances Harris, Miss Dawson," she said in a flat voice.

"Well, give me Cabel. He was supposed to pick me up over half an hour ago!"

Frances's coat was still where she had dropped it, on the chair beside the double doors and she lifted it and draped it over her bare body, clutching it around her with numb fingers. She could hear Cabel slam and check the back door and she waited until he had reached the hallway before she spoke. "The phone's for you, Cabel. I'll see you around."

Her hand was already opening the door, and Cabel's startled pause gave her time to escape. She heard him call after her, heard the door behind her open, and as she ran down the hill, gravity aiding her flight, she heard him call after her, "Frances, damn it, come back here! Frances!"

The rest of the weekend passed like a bad dream, leaving Frances with an unpleasant feeling of disappointment and hopelessness that was as foreign to her nature as the regime she put herself through to avoid him until she could come to terms with herself.

She threw a few things into a bag, called and made arrangements to drop off Tripod with Margaret Shober. Next she called her old college roommate, whom she saw infrequently, although the two of them kept in contact with calls and cards, and then she drove to Winston-Salem.

It was almost eleven when she pulled into Racine's apartment complex and by that time, she had her story pretty well intact. Her rings were removed, the jade ring worn on her right hand and the gold band tucked into a corner of her satin jewel pouch, and she dropped her overnighter on Racine's yellow shag carpet and announced that she was in need of two full days of rest and relaxation, with no questions asked.

She got it. She toured Old Salem, the restored Moravian settlement where she bought tinware, pottery, and Moravian sugar cake; then she spent the afternoon going through an enormous, impressive tobacco manufacturing plant where she grew accustomed to the sweet pungent smell as she followed an attractive guide across the acres of polished hardwood floors that supported row upon row of immensely sophisticated machinery. She managed to smile and nod and look suitably impressed at the handsome, comfortable-looking facilities for the workers.

Afterward, she remembered practically nothing of what she had seen or heard, but she was totally exhausted, and after a swim in the apartment pool, Racine went out for barbecue sandwiches, and they watched television until Frances's eyes began to close.

No questions. Racine was a nurse now, and if she

read anything in Frances's pale face and shadowy eyes, she kept her own counsel.

"Look, Fan, I've got to go on duty at three, so why don't we have a late breakfast and walk through Reynolda Gardens? None of the shops will be open, but the gallery opens at two, and then you can stay on as long as you want while I scram on over to the hospital?"

They more or less followed that plan, with both of them driving, since it was just after twelve by the time they finished a swim and brunch. Racine refrained from questioning her friend, although when she caught Frances's glance on a couple of uninhibited Wake Forest students who paused in a secluded section of the handsome gardens for a long kiss, she sighed rather heavily.

"Honey, anytime you need to get away, I'm here. Old See-No, Hear-No, Speak-No-Racine. But if you want to talk, then I'm available, too, and—count on it—it won't be anything I haven't heard before. Nurses come in for some confidences that would make a soap opera pale in comparison."

With masterfully poor timing, she found herself heading home on an autumn Sunday afternoon along with everyone else who had been to Lake Norman or perhaps the Blue Ridge Parkway, only an hour away and at its loveliest. At least the traffic kept her mind occupied on the hour-and-a-half drive back to Bynum.

Never one for self-searching, Frances nevertheless was forced to come to terms with herself during the few days immediately following her hollow mockery of a wedding ceremony. And what she discovered came as no real surprise to her. Rather, it was almost a relief, as if the doctor had confirmed the suspected presence of a chronic disease, and now all she had to do was learn to live with the knowledge instead of the aching, nameless dread that had nibbled away her inner resources.

She had to come to terms with the knowledge that she was irrevocably in love with Cabel; then she had to put that knowledge on the shelf, where she might allow herself to glance at it once or twice as she went about the business of reconstructing her life.

Unfortunately, what worked in theory didn't hold up so well in actual practice. When Cabel dropped by Frances's house after work on her second day at the Bronze P'ou, she was unable to keep herself from devouring him with her eyes. She had been home long enough to change into a soft, full-length jersey caftan of cinnamon, black, and gold print that doubled as a bathrobe, but Cabel was still in his fine herringbone three-piece suit, the waistcoat unbuttoned and his tie twisted awry so that he could open the top buttons of his creamy shirt.

He sprawled in her one comfortable chair, legs extended before him and shoved a hand through the fitted cap of dark hair. "What a day! There are more schemes for breaking Wall Street than Las Vegas ever dreamed of, and every single instant-expert walked through my doors today. Legalities, morals, ethics—they all fly out the window when one of the have-nots thinks he sees a way to become a have."

"What about when one of the haves wants to become a have-more?"

He slanted her a quizzical look. "Not you, too! You think the world of Oriental art is inscrutable . . . try the wonderful world of high finance sometime and see if you can find your way out of the maze."

"Would you care for a drink?" Frances offered.

"Hmmm. Tempting, but what I'd really like is a needle-sharp shower and then twelve solid hours of sleep. Meanwhile, how are things going for you?"

"Just fine, if you mean the Bronze P'ou. It's marvelous to be surrounded by netsukes and Shiwan Ware and jades and ivories. It even smells exotic, and there's so much I didn't know, even after a minor in Oriental Art." She told him about the consignment of antique blue pottery from Jaipur she had unpacked just that day, and then, noticing the droop of his eyelids, she grinned unselfconsciously and allowed her voice to taper off.

The click of the furnace cutting in seemed to rouse him, and he sat up straighter, flexing his shoulders so that she wished she had the nerve to lay her hands on those tired muscles and work them loose again. "Hope you haven't made any plans for tomorrow night," he said, looking around at her extremely limited space with what almost looked like longing.

"Nothing I can think of. Why?"

"Good. Client of mine . . . nice fellow, you'll like him; coming into Raleigh-Durham Airport at seven tomorrow evening and I want to bring them . . . his wife's along, too . . . out here for a solid dose of Southern hospitality. Think you and Hazel can manage between you?"

Startled, she asked, "Just what did you have in mind?"

"Oh, nothing splashy. Just a comfortable, quiet, family-type affair that will help persuade him to move down here where, incidentally, he'll probably decide to locate a multimillion dollar plant he's planning to build. The choice lies between Piedmont, North Carolina and West Virginia, and another of my clients has an option on some property that might be just what he's looking for."

"All that reeks of . . . well, something or other," Frances accused doubtfully, pressing her back against the intricate scrolls of the bentwood rocker.

"Now that's a peculiar choice of words," Cabel snorted, wrenching himself upright in the upholstered chair. "The fact is, the sale of the property will enable the owner to invest in a small company he owns that's in danger of going out of business and taking some two hundred jobs down the drain with it, plus the fact that the plant, if it's built here, will employ a hell of a lot of local labor in the building stage and then provide even more jobs once it's finished, none of which strikes me as being particularly reprehensible! If there's a profit to be made along the way, it will no doubt be invested in still more expansion, which will provide more jobs."

"And you, just incidentally, will take a commission on it all," she retorted, wondering why she was baiting him this way.

One hand went to stroke the back of his neck. "Look, Frances, I'm not about to defend myself to you. I deal in a variety of investments. It's not a dirty word, believe it or not, and either you trust in my integrity or you don't. If you don't . . ." He shrugged and she wanted above all to take back her snide remark, wanted even more to be able to see the expression on his averted face.

"I'm sorry, Cabel. I do trust you. I couldn't . . ." She was about to say she couldn't have fallen in love with him without that trust, but she changed in the middle of the sentence. "I couldn't begin to understand the intricacies of high finance."

The smile he gave her was twisted, offering a wary acceptance of her apology. "You might call me a tour guide, then. Not too many people do understand even the simple fundamentals of investing."

He stood and walked over to her front window to stare down at the restless river. The trees now were mostly blackened skeletons, a few wearing patches of lurid scarlet or yellow, having been stripped of their finery prematurely by a severe wind and rain the day before. "For your information," he remarked to the window pane as Frances followed the lines of his body with her eyes, "I'll get a modest commission on the land if it's sold; nothing at all on the plant, if it's built. Now . . . about tomorrow night?"

"How long will they be here and what do you want me to do?"

Chapter Eight

"As to the first, I expect they'll be staying about three or four days. I thought we'd have a quiet dinner at home the first night and then plan something a little more ambitious the next. Ed's fed up with the social round, and I'd like to show him that we can be just as social with none of the pressure he's accustomed to in the circles he moves in. Perhaps you'd invite your family for the dinner party."

"My family?"

"Might be a good way to follow up those few minutes after the ceremony. Reassure them that little Fancey's all set so that they can stop worrying. After all, we haven't seen them lately."

"It's been all of what . . . ? Four days? They'd naturally expect us to be honeymooning," Frances snapped, irritated by his bland composure.

"Hmmm. There is that aspect, I suppose. By the way, Mrs. McCloud, where'd you go on your honeymoon?"

She studied him, trying to fathom his mood and could discern nothing beneath the surface pleasantness. "I went to Winston-Salem," she told him.

"Which one of your team of Irishmen enjoyed your company, the traveling salesman or the bow tie?"

Bristling, she retorted, "Have I asked you which one of your mistresses you honeymooned with? But then, I don't have to . . . Miss Dawson was the lucky winner, I believe!" She would have given anything to have remained calm and aloof, but the pain swamped her all over again and it was all she could do to remain seated in the same room with him.

"About that call, Frances," Cabel began, but she cut him off.

"Forget it! We laid out the ground rules before we ever drew up the contract for this partnership, and I'm certainly not complaining. Now . . . my first duty will be this dinner tomorrow night . . . nothing fancy, you said, just a quiet relaxing evening. What about the next day? What will Mrs. . . . ?"

"Moultrie. Ed and Miriam Moultrie," Cabel filled in.

"Right. I assume he'll be with you, but what about his wife? I'll be at work, so I can't look after her."

"We'll work something out, never mind. I haven't met the lady so I haven't a clue what will suit her. And about the next night, how about inviting your sisters and their husbands, your mother, of course, and the aunt and uncle form Durham and . . . let's see . . . we'll need another man to make up numbers so . . . why not invite your two Irishmen and I'll invite Olivia to fill out the table. Suit you?"

She could have strangled him! This was going to be difficult enough without having every move she made examined by those ice-blue Dawson eyes. And for that matter, she could do without Sean and Doyle in attendance. "The menu," she mentioned, forcing herself to go beyond the problems presented by the company alone. "Will you want Beef Wellington and buttered artichokes or . . . ?"

"Make it one of those delectable, high cholesterol Southern specialties . . . maybe roast pork, country ham, red-eye gravy and grits, and biscuits with butterbeans and . . . oh . . . you know the drill."

She had to smile. "Sounds as if you know it pretty well, too," she allowed.

"I'm a quick study," he said modestly, rising and stretching his shoulders tiredly. Frances wondered briefly, painfully, just how much of his tiredness came from his work, but she stood briskly and saw him to the door.

"I just hope Hazel is up to all this, because I'll be at work all day," she said.

"I'll arrange for her to be here full time as long as the Moultries are here," Cabel murmured as he reached for the door. "That way, you can set her a course before you leave in the mornings and check her on it later on, hmmm? I'm sure Olivia won't mind giving her to me for the duration."

I'm sure Olivia wouldn't mind giving you anything you asked for, Frances thought uncharitably, but she kept it to herself. Better not make waves now, of all times. "Good night, Cabel."

"Good night, Mrs. McCloud," he whispered, and before she could step back, he leaned over and laid a sweet, soft kiss on her startled mouth and let himself out.

Before leaving for the airport the next evening, Cabel called in at Frances's house, finding her in the kitchen where she had gone to feed Tripod as soon as she got in from work. The three-legged cat practically inhaled the dish of smelly fishmeal and then flopped an awkward rear end against Frances's leg, tail aquiver as it purred in appreciation.

"Look, it occurs to me that there might be a few awkward questions if my wife hops up after coffee, says good night, all, and takes off. How about bringing over a few things while I'm gone and staying for the duration?"

Nonplussed, she could only stare at him. That aspect of the situation hadn't occurred to her, oddly enough. He hadn't seemed to mind that the housekeeper knew they weren't sharing a house, much less a room, and that, of course, meant that Olivia was aware of the fact, as well.

"There won't be any real problem, will there?" he asked as if impatient to settle the matter and be on his way. "You can run back and forth to look after your cat and then, once the houseparty's over, you're free to take up residence here again."

She didn't know whether to laugh or cry. What an utterly ridiculous situation! His housekeeper knew the truth, his mistress knew the truth, so how on earth had he thought a mere marriage certificate would make a difference? Silly to pretend for a couple of business associates, but if that was what he wanted . . . "If you think it's important," she shrugged. "Does it matter which room? Oh, and where shall I put the Moultries? I thought the room across from yours. It has the best view of the river and the bath's convenient."

"Fine, then you can move into the one next to mine and we'll share my bath. May as well make it look good in case there's any suspicion. I expect your mother will want to get you off into a corner for a little female heart-to-heart, so we'll leave the connecting door open and make her romantic heart flutter a little faster, shall we?" His grin was easy, a friendly thing with no overtones at all and he left without giving Frances a chance to disagree.

If he only knew, she thought, watching his lean, rangey figure slide in under the wheel of his car. Patsy would be hard pressed to understand a marriage that didn't center around a big double bed where all arguments were settled, all problems talked over and the news of the day capped off before a good-night kiss. Frances had heard her parents' voices mumbling through their bedroom door for years, whenever her father, who had been a tobacco auctioneer with a circuit to travel, was home.

By the time Cabel returned with the Moultries, Frances and Hazel between them had contrived a creditable meal and Frances had put fresh flowers in the main rooms. She had ordered them earlier in bulk and arranged them herself while Hazel put the finishing touches in the dining room.

In spite of all her efforts to be pleasant to the slatternly housekeeper, the atmosphere between the two of them was uncomfortable. Frances's position was undermined by the fact that Hazel knew very well she had not lived with her husband since their marriage, and if the woman was capable of any loyalty at all, it was to Olivia Dawson. Her attitude toward Frances was one of ill-concealed contempt, and there wasn't a thing Frances could do about it. Cabel hadn't married her to disrupt his household arrangements, but to improve them, and as things were, that simply didn't seem possible.

Meanwhile, there was tonight to get through. She had put her things in the room that adjoined Cabel's, noticing with more wistfulness than amusement the open door between them, and changed into something she considered suitable for a quiet evening at home with a middle-aged couple. The tie-silk print of blue, lavender, and jade brought a warmth to her face, and she repeated the lavender very subtly in her eye shadow, glancing unconsciously at the jade ring as if to assure herself it was really there. It had been a total surprise, the ring, and she had protested Cabel's spending so much money on her in the circumstances, but he had cut off her argument with a freezing look.

"All I can say is, it ain't no time to go eatin' supper. Eight thirty, nine o'clock! I won't be here to wash no dishes an' I can tell you right now, I don't like comin' into no dirty kitchen first thing in the mornin'," Hazel announced as Frances made one last trip to the kitchen before going to the front door to greet the arrivals.

"You won't have to, Hazel," she told the disgruntled housekeeper quietly. "I'll see that everything's cleared away tonight before I go to bed."

"Hmmmph!" The woman cast her a knowing look from dull, colorless eyes and flounced into the dining room to bring back a heavy cut-glass water pitcher for filling.

There was no time to set her straight . . . nothing to set straight, anyway. Perhaps once this visit was over, she might look around for someone else, and Olivia be damned. If Cabel expected her to oversee his household, he'd have to allow her a certain amount of freedom, especially as he couldn't give her any amount of authority as his wife, at least where Hazel and Olivia Dawson were concerned.

The Moultries were a surprise. At least the distaff side was, for Miriam Moultrie was at least twenty years younger than her tired-looking husband. When the three of them entered the foyer, with Frances to greet them and Hazel to take their bags, the tall, slender platinum blond cast a measuring look around her before she returned Frances's greeting with a perfunctory one of her own—minus the smile.

Ed Moultrie made up for his wife's lack of friendliness by his genuine interest in the house, the area, and the food, which was plain fried chicken and garden vegetables. The okra intrigued him, and Frances hoped his obvious appreciation would make up for his wife's derisive comments as she pushed around the small servings and made do with several glasses of the excellent wine Cabel had selected. Hazel was getting ready to leave when Frances went to the kitchen for the coffee and the older woman announced flatly, and in an embarrassingly loud voice, "That man done ate like a horse, he did, and she didn't do no more than mess her plate up."

"Yes, well, it was delicious, Hazel. Mrs. Moultrie evidently had something on the flight so that she wasn't really all that hungry."

The housekeeper slammed out the back door, mumbling something about going back to them that liked her ways, and Frances wished heartily that she'd make good her threat.

Shortly after they had coffee, Ed Moultrie said

137

good-night and Frances expected his wife to accompany him. But instead, Miriam looked at Cabel, a speculative light in her light gray eyes, and announced that she needed some exercise after the flight to put her in a mood to sleep.

There was nothing Cabel could do, Frances told herself as she watched him escort the lovely blond out the front door, except offer to accompany her on a walk down to the river. The fact that the moon would be rising within half an hour or so was an added inducement, and Frances began clearing away the dining room with an impatience that only partly disguised the hurt she was feeling. Miriam tonight, Olivia tomorrow night . . . if it was variety Cabel wanted, then he had arranged his affairs perfectly, only Frances wouldn't be part of that variety.

She blew an escaping wisp of hair off her forehead and plunged the last pan into the tired suds half an hour later. Cabel and Miriam were still out there somewhere, with Cabel no doubt exercising that exasperating, fascinating charm of his on the all too willing blond. It looked as if business took second place as far as he was concerned, for surely he didn't expect Ed Moultrie to be too happy about the situation.

There was satisfaction to be gained from scouring the crust from the frying pan, and long after the surface was scrubbed clean, Frances glowered at the steamy window over the sink and rubbed the copper bottom in vigorous time with her angry thoughts. It would serve him right if she walked out flat and left him to explain her absence as best he could. Nice family affair, my foot! Cabel's idea of a family affair was an affair with someone else's family! Namely, his client's wife! If she hadn't already invited her own family for dinner tomorrow night, she'd walk out right now, but that would take more explaining than she was capable of. Still, it might be amusing to watch them . . . Olivia and Miriam, Cabel and Doyle, with poor old Sean left to entertain her, no doubt!

"May I ask what you're mumbling about?" Cabel asked from behind her. She hadn't even heard him come in and now she whirled around, looking past him to the empty hallway.

"What happened to your guest, or did you put her back under her rock?" she asked, and then could have bit off her tongue.

"My, we're awfully testy tonight, aren't we? Are you already dissatisfied with your working conditions? Ready to renegotiate your contract?" It was as though he wanted her to flare up, as if he were taunting her deliberately. Contrarily, she refused to be baited.

"Not at all," she replied calmly. "Perhaps Mrs. Moultrie would like me to run her bath for her . . . unless you've already offered," she added with saccharine sweetness.

"Now what can Miriam Moultrie have done to put you in this interesting frame of mind, I wonder," Cabel mused. "You sound almost as if you were jealous, but that's too farfetched, I suppose." He slanted her a querying look as he leaned back against the counter and fondled a cold pipe in his hand.

"Don't be ridiculous! I'm going up to bed," Frances announced, flinging the damp dish towel across the rack impatiently. Cabel's words had struck home and she didn't like dealing with herself in this mood.

"Sounds like a good idea," he replied with a benign smile.

"Alone!"

He levered himself away from the cabinet, switching off the light, and followed her across the broad gleaming expanse of polished pine floors. "Sorry you had to clean up all this mess. Maybe I should have asked Hazel to sleep over."

"Don't bother! I'd rather wash up after a regiment than put up with any more of her snide remarks."

"That bad, hmm?" He took her arm and steered her into the living room, and the teasing look was gone from his face as he seated her on the down-cushioned sofa. The coals of an earlier fire still glowed on the hearth and the room seemed warm and welcoming as the tiredness of the long, difficult day suddenly caught up with her.

Wordlessly, she stared back at him, too weary to care any more. It was as if the comfortable cushions drained her of the dregs of anger, jealousy, and hopelessness, leaving behind only an emptiness, waiting to be filled.

Cabel knocked his pipe out on the tile-faced fireplace and left it on the mantel before joining her on the sofa. Even then, he didn't touch her. Over the subtle scent of the apple wood that had taken the chill off the evening, she was aware of his cologne, a light, mossy fragrance that was almost not there, coupled with the odor of good woolens and aromatic tobacco. She stiffened herself against the imperceptible spell he could cast without even trying.

"Now," he said, turning to face her, "What's the trouble? All of it."

"In alphabetical order?" she quipped, trying for lightness and failing.

"Try starting with Hazel."

"All right, I will. She's dreadful! She knows very

140

well I don't . . . I mean, we don't . . . and, well, she makes remarks."

"I take it you're referring to our rather unorthodox marriage arrangements. Hmmmm. Well, unless you're willing to really get into the part . . . for Hazel's benefit, that is, I don't see what I can do about it."

Getting wound up by now, Frances continued, leaning forward in order to press on him the seriousness of her charges. "And you know very well that what Hazel knows, Olivia knows," she pointed out, "so where's the value of our marriage? I might just as well have stayed home!"

"Except for the Moultries."

"Not that a little thing like a wife kept that woman from throwing herself at you," she charged sulkily. "And you standing there with a catcher's mitt on! What do you suppose poor Ed thought?"

Unexpectedly, he grinned. "If it's of any comfort to you, wife, she struck out, thanks to you. I'm afraid Miriam's the sort to get up to mischief whenever possible and I let her know in the kindest sort of way that my hands were full with my new bride."

"You didn't!" Frances crowed, suddenly feeling quite revived.

With a modest, if somewhat smug smile, Cabel nodded. "I'm not about to endanger the whole deal before it ever gets off the ground, so I thought I'd better get things straight in the beginning. What better way than to walk in the moonlight with one woman while I sing the praises of another?"

"Cabel! Did you really?"

"Scout's honor. You wouldn't have recognized yourself, Fancey, by the time I got through spreading it on."

The smile faded from her face. "Thanks for the vote of confidence," she jeered.

He gave her a measuring look that puzzled her and she reluctantly lowered a tucked-up foot to the floor and made as if to rise. With one hand, he stayed her. "What's the matter, Frances? The cards-on-the-table approach beginning to pall?" It was an easy matter to tip her back against the cushions, and he followed the action with a finger on her lip, a finger that pressed insinuatingly as his eyes began to speak.

Frances moved abruptly. The spell of the firelight, the almost overwhelming silence in the large old house, and the nearness of this man were confusing her, beguiling her, and she could ill-afford to be beguiled. His every word, every look, was open to misinterpretation in her present state of mind, and she tried for matter-of-factness when she suggested that he lean the fire screen up against the fireplace before he came upstairs.

"Frances?" he persisted softly, ignoring her words. "We could make things more convincing to the Moultries . . . to Hazel, too, if it matters."

In the face of her dismayed confusion, he persisted. "Why not?" He traced a line from her nose to her lips, her chin, and down her throat, meandering slowly into the shadowy valley between her breasts. "You can't deny you're attracted to me, and I haven't any objection to . . . shall we say, normalizing the situation between us?"

His smile was whimsical, a flashing of that lopsided dimple, a showing of strong white teeth, but his eyes were in shadow, unreadable in the dim light of the lamp behind them. Frances drew back and stared at him strickenly. If he had deliberately set out to prevent any such thing from happening, he couldn't have gone about it any more efficiently. She hid the bitter medicine of her dissappointment with a brittle facade. "Careful, there. You might be getting in over your head. For all you know, I could take you up on it and then you'd be in trouble." She managed a parody of a smile and was thankful for the dimness of the lighting. "We agreed . . . no pretense between us, remember?"

With a lightninglike change of moods, Cabel withdrew, clamping his hands on his widespread, muscular thighs. "What the hell do you think I'm pretending? Can't you accept the fact that I'd like to sleep with my own wife, for God's sake?"

"No, as a matter of fact, I can't! Oh, I'm not saying it might not be the truth, but let's get something straight, Cabel; you can do your . . . your womanizing somewhere else. I'm not interested in adding my scalp to your collection, and now if you'll excuse me, I have a big day tomorrow."

She twisted herself to a standing position, her head lifted high enough to disguise the beginning of tears as she stared down at him. Lord, was ever a man worth all the pain? She hated him, hated him for making her love him and even now, knowing he was simply passing time with her, she was tempted!

"All things considered, Frances, I think I've been pretty patient with you," he gritted out. She thought fleetingly that he looked . . . baffled, somehow. "Anytime you're ready to face facts and straighten out this stupid state of affairs between us, I'll be waiting, but you'll have to come to me. I can't fight your defenses any longer," he finished tiredly.

Taking a deep, steadying breath, she said, "In the first place, there is no affair to be straightened out between us, nor will there be. In the second place, the basic ground rules have been spelled out so that even a dimwit like myself can read them; and in the third place, Cabel McCloud, after this Moultrie debacle, I think it's about time we started working on our annulment! I'll hostess this one thing for you, but as for taking on your household, I can't work with your mistress's housekeeper! I'd advise you to take on the pair of them! Between them, they'll set you up in fine shape, but from now on, leave me out of it!" She whirled to go and he caught her at the base of the stairs.

"All right, you dried-up shrew, you've had your say, and now you're going to listen while I have mine! I married you when you needed a husband. Wait!" He held up a silencing hand when she would have flung his charge back at him. "Let me finish and then you can complain all you want to, I won't be here to hear it! I gave you my name and secured your job for you so that you could keep that squatter's shanty you call a home, and you think I'd trade off my freedom for one dinner party? Lady, I don't come that cheap!"

The glitter in his eyes was like nothing she had ever seen before, and she drew back, unable to break away completely from the raw, unleashed power of him. Somewhere in the back of her mind there flickered a thought about his need for a wife to stand between him and the more importunate of his female friends, but his hard-driving voice chased all other thoughts from her mind as he continued speaking.

"There'll be two more things I'll require of you before I turn you loose and then you can go to the devil for all I care! The Moultries leave day after tomorrow. The next day is Friday and you can make plans to go with me to Nassau for the weekend."

She opened her mouth to protest, but he ignored

her, washing over her puny resistance like a tidal wave. "We're meeting someone there and you're going to turn in an award-winning performance as a devoted wife or I'll make you know what being a real wife means! And what's more," his eyes narrowed as he raked her from head to toe, "you know exactly what I mean, don't you?"

A wheezy old clock struck eleven-thirty, and still they glared at each other. Frances's hands were clutching her stomach as if the pain that shafted through her body had an actual physical source. But Cabel's hands remained at his sides, his fingers curled into his palms so tightly that his knuckles showed white, as if he were fighting a desire to strike her.

Without another word, Frances turned and made her way up the stairs, each step measured and leaden as she moved like an unfeeling automaton toward the scant security of her room.

The next day finally passed after what seemed thirty-six hours. Not even the exquisite consignment of jadeite carvings that came in could lift her spirits, and Frances stood by the window of the Bronze P'ou and rubbed a pendant absently, while her mind drifted back to the house on the hill.

Her eyes felt dry and gritty from lack of sleep, but sleep had been impossible after she closed the door behind her. The communicating door had stood mockingly open, for one thing, and thanks to the aged, sloping floors, the only way she had been able to secure it had been to place a chair under the knob. There had been a slight satisfaction in hearing him striding about as he got ready for bed, slamming drawers with no consideration for the guests just across the hall, much less the wife on the other side of the paneled door. At least he wasn't indifferent to her, whatever else he wasn't.

With the dinner party irrevocably scheduled for seven tonight, Frances wasn't allowed the privilege of temperament. She had gone directly to the kitchen this morning as soon as she heard Hazel's noisy attendance, and given her orders for the day, ignoring the smug, malicious looks. Then she crossed the hall for her coat, intent on escaping before Cabel came downstairs.

But her plan was thwarted. He appeared at the bottom of the stairs to tell her that Miriam had agreed to join him and Ed for the morning. "I'll turn her over to my secretary and then, after lunch, we'll make some arrangements for shopping, or whatever you women do to pass time in a strange town. Pity you're tied up."

"Yes, isn't it?" she remarked coolly, sliding her arm into her lightweight beige topper. She was thinking, I didn't even know he had a secretary, although only an idiot would suppose otherwise.

"Will you be able to manage tonight?" he asked politely and she said, "Yes, thank you," just as politely.

They stared at each other for several long seconds and then Cabel shook himself and turned away toward the dining room. Frances closed the front door behind her. He hadn't even asked her if she'd had breakfast . . . which she hadn't. He hadn't asked if she'd slept well, either . . . which she hadn't, and from the looks of the gray lines beside his implacable mouth, neither had he.

Oh, God, she cried silently as she ground the starter unmercifully before shooting off down the hill, why can't I just let it flow? Why do I have to freeze up whenever he's around? On paper it looked as if we might have a chance, but we both seem to go crazy whenever we're together for more than five minutes!

That had been this morning. The afternoon had been little better, although she had sold a nineteenth-century Korean rice chest of Zelkovia wood to a collector from Southern Pines who promised to return with his wife, who collected snuff bottles. That had made it easier to ask for Friday off. And when she reminded Mrs. Macheris that she and her husband had never had a proper honeymoon, she was told to take Monday as well, if she wanted it.

She dreaded the party all the way home, but her thoughts about the upcoming weekend trip all but crowded the worries out, and she admitted to herself reluctantly that she was looking forward to being with Cabel somewhere away from all past ties. Perhaps it still wasn't too late. If she had only a hint that his feelings for her went deeper than convenience and a momentary lust, she might find the courage to tell him how she felt.

Chapter Nine

Only the fact that Miriam Moultrie was on hand to watch her performance allowed Frances to get through the time between leaving the Bronze P'ou and greeting the first arrivals. She was dead on her feet, as much from pure tension as from lack of sleep, and the thirty-minute soak as she sipped a glass of Madeira helped less than she had hoped.

Cabel, home early for once, was free to entertain their guests and thus allow her time enough to pull herself together. She paid extraordinary attention to the details of her dress, choosing a plain white silk jersey dinner dress and wearing only her wedding band, her jade ring, and a pair of plain gold earrings. She made up her face carefully in order to disguise the shadows that hollowed her cheekbones and enlarged her eyes, but nothing could hide a strange look of wistfulness. She hoped, as she added a final whiff of Odalesque, that it would be taken as worldly sophistication instead of the vulnerability it actually was. Her shell felt terribly fragile tonight.

Doyle brought Olivia and they and Patsy arrived in a group a few minutes before the others. She was chagrined to see a long white skirt under Olivia's velvet wrap and she couldn't help but glance down at her own dress.

"Honey, you look awful," Patsy announced in ringing tones as she wriggled out of her tweed and squeezed Cabel's arm. It wasn't Cabel she was addressing, however, and Frances brought off a creditable laugh as Doyle mentioned the newlywed state and Olivia glared coldly at her.

Either barrage might have been her undoing had not Cabel taken each woman on an arm and guided them into the living room, leaving Frances to show Doyle where to hang his topcoat.

"Hmm, bloody swank you landed in, Frances. No wonder you didn't have time for a struggling salesman."

"Don't be silly, Doyle. As I remember it, you ditched me as soon as you laid eyes on Olivia Dawson, so don't go crying any crocodile tears. Come on, I'll give you a drink." She suddenly felt on top of the situation. It would be all right, at least as long as her garrulous relatives were reasonably discreet.

From then on, the evening moved forward with a momentum of its own. Her sisters and their husbands arrived with Aunt Helen and Uncle Jerrold and Sean and Jerrold talked of Duke's team while Jean, Kay, and Aunt Helen went over the affairs of the younger generation. Both Kay and Jean had one child each under five, and while Frances adored them both, she could do without hearing about each bite they took and every word they spoke.

Patsy and Ed Moultrie found things to discuss while Cabel stood talking to Olivia. Frances's eyes were drawn again and again to the pair of them as they stood before the fireplace. Cabel looked unusually handsome without half trying, wearing a dark lounge suit and a modestly tucked shirt with a sober tie. The cufflinks he wore were equally sober, but the more elegant for it and from there, Frances moved on to study the sparkling brunette who was holding his attention.

Olivia Dawson would hold any man's attention, she admitted reluctantly. The white dress she wore put Frances's own modest creation in the shade, and the necklace that adorned it was stunning. It had to be real, for the depth of light in those tones could only come from diamonds and the blue central stone, only a few shades darker than Olivia's light blue eyes, was unusual in itself, and set in an intriguing design.

It wasn't until they were seated at the dinner table that Frances began to relax. The Madeira she had sipped in her bath, plus the drink Cabel had handed her when she came downstairs, helped, as did the familiar chatter of her own family, who were oblivious to any undertones.

The dining room gleamed softly, its high ceiling muting the mingled voices, as if filing them away with the residue of the past century or so. The table was long and made of walnut, as were the chairs, and though of no particular style, they were handsome and to Frances's way of thinking, distinctive. She was proud, for Cabel's sake, of the gracious overall effect of the traditional china, silver, and crystal in the dove gray room, and it occurred to her to wonder, not for the first time, how he had come by such possessions.

Not that he couldn't afford them. They had not discussed his financial standing, but it was evident that he was secure enough in his position to enjoy quality without ostentation. Most other moneyed bachelors of her acquaintance would have gone in for an indoor pool, or tennis courts and a sauna, or at the very least, a conference-sized hot tub.

"Hmmmm?" She returned to her surroundings to answer Sean's question and then, as she began to lapse back into her own soft-focused world, she became aware of someone's staring at her. Glancing around, she saw Olivia's marblelike eyes slide away as a secret little smile curled her lips.

Several times during the remainder of the meal, she caught the smug expression, the malicious gleam in eyes that refused to lock with hers, and by the time they rose from the table to have coffee in the living room, Frances was seething again.

The dozen people arranged themselves in small groups and from her vantage point in front of the heavy Georgian coffee service, Frances was able to let her mind flow into the different conversations, satisfying herself that all was well. Milo, Kay's husband, was telling Cabel about the distinctive breed of English setter that had taken all the field trial honors in the early sixties, insisting that Mollie had the right coloring, size, and conformation, and promising to look around for a dog of the same strain if he could have first choice of the pups.

Patsy was proclaiming the advantages of mulching to Ed Moultrie, who probably didn't do all that much gardening in Chicago, and Helen was telling Sean about the daughter of one of Jerrold's teaching friends. Olivia leaned back in the high-backed

Queen Ann chair and gazed openly at Cabel, her eyes moving down the length of him and then back again at a slow simmer. Frances sat her cup down firmly. Determined to try and be civil, she crossed to take the matching chair.

"Miss Dawson, I couldn't help but admire your necklace. It looks handwrought, and I was wondering if the stones were from North Carolina? My father was a rock hound and he found some marvelous blue tourmaline that I've always wanted to have something done with."

Olivia's flawless white hand fluttered up to touch the gleaming arrangement of stones set in what appeared to be free-form cast gold. She leaned forward and said in a low, husky voice brimming with laughter, "I'm sure I don't know where they came from, darling. It was a gift." Her eyes cut to where Cabel stood, engrossed in a conversation with Ed Moultrie, Milo, and Jean's husband, Shelby. "We considered the jade . . . in fact, I think . . . well, of course, that's water over the dam now, isn't it?" Her eyes went meaningfully to Frances's ring. "I love these, though, and of course, they're sapphires, not tourmalines. He wouldn't think of giving me one of the lesser stones."

Somehow, Frances managed to get through the rest of the evening. She must have said all the right things, for Patsy took her aside as she was leaving to compliment her on finally growing up. "You were perfect for this place, Fancey Ann, and I'm not surprised that a man like Cabel saw it right off the bat. I couldn't have done better for you if I'd tried."

The Moultries went upstairs together for a change, and Frances waited until she heard Cabel let himself out the back door for Mollie's last run before making her way to her own room. She leaned against the coolness of the white paneled door and closed her eyes while the pain washed over her in waves.

So what else is new? You knew Olivia's position in his life when you married him. A man doesn't marry his mistress, but that's not to say he doesn't also need a wife in the background. But to bring her here, to flaunt her before Patsy and Kay and Jean . . . ! And that necklace! Had they deliberated together, buying jade and sapphire both? Had Cabel then offered Frances, herself, the leftovers?

She tugged the ring from her finger and threw it across the room. She hadn't asked for an engagement ring in the first place, and to be offered one that another woman had refused was just too much to bear.

She was asleep when he finally came upstairs. Pure exhaustion had taken its toll, and if she roused on hearing a door open quietly, if she stirred restlessly as someone touched her shoulder, it was all forgotten in the morning, like the mist that rose over the river to be dispelled by the warming sun.

There were exactly forty-seven minutes between seeing the Moultries off for Chicago and boarding a plane for Miami and from there to Nassau. Frances had flown before and she had visited several of the low-lying islands along the Carolinas and Georgia, but she had never seen water as intensely blue as that she flew over out of Miami. When the water closer to the gemlike islands shaded into a jade that matched her ring, she rubbed the bare gold band on her left hand unconsciously.

She had brought the jade along with her, for just as she couldn't bear to wear it, she also couldn't

153

leave it behind. There had been little or no time to discuss the matter with Cabel, not that she had any idea what to say to him on the matter, for he had buried himself in a briefcase full of papers when they left Raleigh-Durham and come up for air only when they touched down in Atlanta. He asked her then about the clothes she had brought along. She answered briefly and then they both stared away from each other while tension shimmered between them like a living presence.

Just as Cabel had secured them reservations on connecting flights at a moment's notice, so he whisked them through customs and immigration. Then they were ushered into one of the numerous waiting taxis, leaving Frances with a kaleidoscopic impression of bright, wide smiles, melodious, uninhibited voices, loud shirts and straw hats . . . and the sunshine. Surely the same sun didn't beam down on this ocean island that shone on Chatham County, North Carolina?

After an initial reaction, in which she ducked against Cabel to his amusement, Frances discovered that their taxi driver was no more suicidal than any other, that traffic could flow just as freely and safely on the left-hand as on the more familiar right. Cabel's indulgence was the first sign of anything other than mere politeness between them and against all logic, Frances treasured it. When his arm crossed her shoulder casually as he pointed out a particular view along the narrow, dusty road, she allowed it to remain.

"I'm glad this will be your first taste of the Bahamas," he murmured as they careened along beside a limestone wall, with dusty sage scrub and fluid palms flashing past. "I prefer something more off the beaten track when there's time, but my mother's been here for over a month now and she's anxious to meet you."

"Your mother!" she blurted out, pulling away from that bare arm draped so carelessly over her shoulder. "Why didn't you tell me?"

A grimace flickered across his face and disappeared almost before she recognized it for what it was: Cabel was ill at ease! Somehow, the idea that this enigmatic, often exasperating man she had married in such haste could be anything less than in command of a situation disarmed her completely, and she remained silent during the remainder of the drive to their tall, blindingly white hotel. She had come along with the full intention of telling him what she thought of any man who would flaunt his mistress under the noses of his wife and in-laws, but somehow, there was a sense of unreality about the past few days—about everything that had happened between them so far, in fact. Reality failed to stretch across the hundreds of miles they had traveled, leaving her encapsulated within a fragile, impossibly colorful bubble with this man whose nearness was beginning to have an effect on her breathing.

"We'll talk about it after we check in and loosen the kinks with something tall, cool, and rum-filled. I'd have preferred one of the out islands, at least, but bear with me . . . it'll only be for a weekend."

"Look, Cabel, I'm no blasé world traveler. Frankly, I'm still trying to get over Miami International, so a taste of typical tourist fare won't bore me at all. Is your mother at this hotel?"

"Lord, no!" he paid the fare and handed their bags to a beaming porter whom they followed into the gleaming coolness of the lobby. "Mother's over on Paradise Island. We came to see her, but I have no intention of living in her pocket while we're here. You'll see what I mean when you meet her."

A touch of grimness entered his voice again and Frances slanted a curious look up at him. But when Cabel said later, he meant later, and she followed him meekly to the desk and then to the handsome, impersonal suite he had booked them into.

The flowers were nice. They took away some of that mass-produced, sanitized feeling common to so many chain hotels. But if it were a chain, it was an exclusive chain and Frances wandered about, opening doors and looking out of windows, delighting in the small balcony that was theirs alone. There was one bedroom, with two double beds, but she assumed Cabel would be sleeping on the sofa in the attractive sitting room. Either that, or she would!

"I've had drinks sent up, if you'd like to shower and change into something first. Mother'll be here for dinner . . . her current spouse, as well, I'm afraid. I haven't met this one, so I can't guarantee anything, but . . . well, go and shower. We'll talk over rum punches."

They did. Frances had changed into a summery yellow gauze and she waited, enchanted with the abundance of flowers and glossy green shrubbery around the base of the hotel. Further out was a travel-poster view of the sea, looking like a mosaic of gemstones as it traced the curving beaches of cream-colored sand.

Cabel came through the sliding louvered doors, drops of water glinting on his cap of dark hair. He had changed into white duck pants and a black knit shirt and he dropped down beside her and reached for his drink. "Mother," he said in a baffling tone.

He pursed his lips and lifted expressive brows. "Well, in case I haven't filled you in, my mother left us when I was about five. I didn't see her again until I was ready for prep school, and after that, probably no more than half a dozen times in all. Oh, we kept up with each other. When Dad died, Mother wanted to come, but she was in Mexico getting a divorce and . . . well," he shrugged, "it just didn't work out. This will be the first time I've seen her in about four years."

"But Cabel, how did she know about me?" Frances asked, puzzled over more than just his attitude toward his mother.

"I called to tell her we were getting married . . . not to invite her, you understand." A sardonic twist of his mouth appeared as he gazed out over the coral-tinted sky. "Lord, I can see it now, Mother and Patsy exchanging views on the holy state of matrimony."

Frances stiffened, suspecting a slight to her own family, but Cabel quickly put her straight on that score. "I wouldn't have subjected Patsy to my mother for the world, Frances. Nor you, either, until I had time to prepare you."

"But why now?" she asked, meaning why now that our marriage is already grinding to a halt?

Again that lift of a shoulder. "You had to meet her sooner or later, I suppose. May as well get it over with. Besides, I owe the woman something. She gave me my first taste of what marriage could be like, seeing her and my father together when I was too young to realize what was going on, and then seeing my father trying his damndest to recover from what she did to him."

A fragrant breeze lifted the hair from her neck,

157

and she heard sounds of laughter, traffic, and music. She felt as if she were someone else; not the Frances who had tramped the red hills of home, collecting dried weeds from the edges of fields of millet, corn, and tobacco not long ago.

"What are you thinking?" Cabel asked unexpectedly.

She told him, adding that she was afraid she was a dyed-in-the-wool provincial. "I'll embarrass you, just you wait. I want to stare at everything and then taste it, touch it, or smell it to be sure it isn't plastic. Imagine flowers that size growing this time of the year! It's . . . it's indecent!"

He laughed and some of the tension seemed to ease from his face, making her aware for the first time that it had been there, under the seemingly casual description of his relationship with his mother. He might think he wasn't still affected by her, but Frances had a new insight into this man she had married, and it brought with it certain doubts. Lord knows, she couldn't afford to start looking beneath his deceptively attractive surface now, not when she had made up her mind to leave him as soon as they reached home again.

For that matter, he had as good as told her he had had enough, which made it all the more puzzling, this meeting with his estranged mother.

"It'll be another hour and a half before we meet for dinner, if you'd like a nap," he offered.

"Hmmmm, I don't know. I think I'll just sit out here and watch the sun splash down, if that's all right."

"Suit yourself. I have some calls to make, so if you'll excuse me . . . ?"

There was a perfectly good telephone in the suite,

but Cabel chose to go elsewhere to make his calls, leaving Frances to wonder if he was trying to prepare his mother to meet her. In the end, she did lie down on one of the beds and managed to doze until he roused her to dress for dinner.

It was a little tricky, getting bathed and dressed with the one bedroom and bath between them and Frances bit back a remark about the accommodations. No doubt, Cabel was expecting his mother to visit their rooms sooner or later, and he was only trying to prevent any embarrassing questions.

In spite of a feeling of distaste for it, Frances wore the white jersey again, for her selection of resort wear was limited. She was fastening on her gold earrings when Cabel wandered out into the bedroom, looking unfairly handsome in his white linen, and Frances wondered when, if ever, she could learn to remain unaffected by him.

"Where's your ring?" he demanded, suddenly coming to a halt just behind her.

She stared at his reflection in consternation. This was no time to go into the matter of her engagement ring, not when they were expected downstairs in a matter of minutes. "I . . . it's in my dressing case."

"Why aren't you wearing it?"

There was no escaping the compulsion of his eyes and she found herself mumbling something about the fit, but he ordered her to get the ring.

"Really, Cabel, I think I can manage to select my jewelry without your help," she declared, fumbling with the backs of the nugget-shaped earrings.

"Here, let me do that," he said gruffly, taking the tiny part from her and pushing her head down at an angle.

His touch was electric, especially in the sensitive

area just below her ear, and when he secured the backing onto the post and let his fingers trail across her exposed nape, she shuddered involuntarily.

"Why aren't you wearing it, Frances?" he asked gravely.

There was nothing to do but answer him. When she told him that she refused to wear a ring he had initially purchased for another woman, his fingers bit into her shoulders with a force that would leave marks for days to come.

"God! You don't pull your punches, do you?" he demanded fiercely.

"Cabel, you're hurting me!"

"I ought to strangle you!" he threatened, but his grasp eased, all the same. "What the hell gave you the idea that I bought that ring with anyone but you in mind?"

"Well, you might say I got it straight from the horse's mouth!" She attempted a brittleness that would mask the bitterness she felt, but when Cabel turned her to him roughly, glaring down into her face as if he intended to rip the truth from her, no matter what, she told him frankly. "Your . . . friend, Olivia, said that the two of you considered both the jade and the sapphires you gave her before discarding the jade. I suppose you thought it was a shame to waste it, after she decided she liked the necklace better, but really, Cabel, I'd have been happier with just the band. I'd have been happier with nothing at all, if you want the plain truth!" she finished angrily, as her voice betrayed her by its unevenness.

Pushing an unsteady hand through his hair, Cabel turned away from her, his shoulders lifting and falling as he expelled an exasperated breath. "Oh boy, what timing. We really manage to stage these things beautifully, don't we?" he jeered softly, turning to her with a look she found impossible to interpret. "Look, Frances, if it matters to you, I . . ."

"But it doesn't!" she interrupted brightly, swallowing against a painful lump that had arisen in her throat. "It doesn't matter at all, so why make a federal case out of it? If you think I look like a poor relation without any more jewelry, then pick me a flower. I'll wear it over my ear! Let's see," she raced on feverishly, turning away to hide the sudden brilliance that shimmered in her eyes, "which is the proper ear for a married woman? But then, that wouldn't do either, would it?"

He exploded. "Frances, shut up! Come here to . . ."

"Oh, you finally lost an argument to me, didn't you?" she taunted. "Remember what you said about . . . ?"

"I remember what I said, all right," he growled, "only I never said enough! Well, maybe now's the time to set the record straight, Frances McCloud." He reached for her and she evaded him, anger trembling away into something far more dangerous.

"There's no time to argue with you, but there's time enough for this!" he promised, as he captured her by the wrist and swung her into his arms.

No sign of gentleness now, nothing but hard, frustrated anger as he forced her head back and took his fill of her stubbornly closed lips. "Open your mouth, Frances. You'll not deny me this time if you know what's good for you."

"Oh, we're resorting to threats now, are we? Well, you made another threat when you ordered me to come on this trip with you, Cabel, and if you think you're going to get away with treating me like . . . like you would one of your . . . your women, then you can think again!" His arms were crushing her against him, making her stunningly aware of the masculine force of him, inflaming her against all her resistance, and she could have wept at the weakness of her pitiful defenses.

Magically, his voice poured over her trembling senses, like melted chocolate over gravel, and she became aware of a change in the way he was holding her. "I don't want to treat you like one of my women, Fancey. I want to treat you like my wife," he whispered, while his hands stroked the silken lines of her body. He lowered his mouth to hers again, slowly this time, as his glowing eyes dared her to refuse him.

Her mouth met his like a flower meets the sun, opening and coming to a fullness that was inevitable. The pure mastery of his hold on her was irresistible and she gave in to the demands of her own body, accomodating herself to him as he shaped her closer to his blatant masculine strength.

His fingers were in her hair, her ears, touching her breasts and running sinuously down her flanks to cup under the roundness of her hips. When the phone shrilled against the shimmering emotional tension that held them suspended in time and space, she crumpled against him with a small whimper.

"Oh God," he groaned, holding her away from him with trembling hands. There was a curious vulnerability about him that struck to the core of her as she watched him struggle for control. When he crossed the room to bark into the receiver, she leaned her weight on the dresser, her head falling onto her chest as she willed her heart to behave.

Quit crying for the moon, she pleaded silently. What he offers is not enough and you'd be better off without ever knowing what it is you'll be aching for all the rest of your life. A simple kiss can play havoc enough with your common sense; Lord knows what it would do to you to have him make love to you in the fullest sense!

Katherine McCloud Beal came as a complete surprise. Frances wondered if she even remembered all those names in between, as she touched the heavily veined, perfectly manicured hand that was extended and quickly withdrawn.

They had met in the lobby and gone on to a nearby restaurant instead of stopping in the hotel dining room, and on the short ride, Frances had had plenty of time to study her as she kept up a line of stiff inconsequential chatter with her son.

About fifty-five, Frances concluded, although that would have made her awfully young when her son was born. She looked both older and younger than her probable age, and Frances concluded that it was due to expert cosmetic surgery that gave her face that masklike look, as well as the most expensive salon treatments available. The pale mink she wore despite the balmy weather matched her hair perfectly. And her clothes, even to Frances's relatively unschooled eyes, were definitely top-drawer designer, one-of-a-kind, and they fit her tiny, fragile figure with a kindness that disguised the lack of any feminine curves.

Much later, she learned that Katherine had fought a recurring battle with alcohol that had left her little more than a husk, but a glamorous husk it was, and Frances was more than a little in awe of the woman that first night.

Tony Beal was somewhere in his late forties, she surmised, and addicted to drink, rich food, and probably a few other things. He admitted to having spent the past eight nights at a casino and added facetiously, with an overdone wink at Francès, that he was glad he had been coerced into coming along to meet his new family.

Cabel's distaste for the man was barely disguised, and it increased over the next few hours, as Tony grew more and more familiar with his new daughter-in-law several times removed. It was impossible to judge Katherine's reaction to her husband's philandering, for her jaded eyes, so like Cabel's in color, if in nothing else, seemed to be permanently and bitterly amused at the world in general.

They finished the peppery conch chowder, and the grilled grouper. By the time Frances sampled the tiny sugar bananas Cabel insisted she try while the Beals had still another drink, she was ready to leave. More than ready, for she had met Katherine and that was the main purpose of the trip, and the meeting had left her feeling terribly sorry for both Cabel and his mother. Katherine Beal was one of the most unhappy people she had ever met, and Cabel . . . well, any unhappiness Cabel had felt at the desertion by his mother had gradually sunk deeply into his innermost self, and was long since covered by layers of urbanity, each a little more polished than the last, all serving to leave him impervious to the hurt a women could inflict on a man.

The compulsive rhythm of drums and electric guitars followed them out into the incredibly soft night air, mingling with other music from other sources. And when Tony offered to show Frances the straw market, the shopping arcade, and the casinos while Cabel and Katherine visited together the next day, she declined quickly, without even waiting for Cabel's opinion.

They said good-night and Cabel invited her to walk along the beach before turning in.

Wary of the witchery of the island, she hesitated. "Perhaps we'd better save it for tomorrow," she stalled.

He took her hand and led her to where a dark-faced Bahamian waited smilingly beside his taxi. "You may be able to sleep after a meal like that, but I'd have nightmares from the chowder alone. The stuff was the color of gunpowder."

Allowing herself to be drawn along, she laughed shakily. "It was pretty well-seasoned, but I enjoyed it. Have you ever had clam chowder at Hatteras? It's got almost as much pepper . . . they leave out the milk and use mostly clam juice with onions, potatoes, and fried bits of salt pork . . . and the clams, of course."

They discussed the food, but Frances's mind was not on what they had dined on, and she had a strong idea Cabel was no more interested in the comparative cuisine than she was. His fingers threaded through hers as the driver accepted payment from him and bade them good-night in a melodious Bahamian accent. Frances told herself she was imagining that knowing lilt in his voice.

They didn't mention Katherine at all. They didn't speak until they both stood barefooted at the edge of the surf, with the stored warmth of the sun seeping into their bones like an insidious invitation to stretch out on the soft sands. "Look at me, Frances," Cabel murmured against the whisper of the water.

Compulsively, she obeyed him, tilting her head up so that the fullness of the moon shone on her face. If he had eyes to see, he could read her heart there, for she was beyond dissembling; far beyond anything at this moment. The night, the island, the seductive perfume of exotic flowers—all combined to rob her of any defense against his overwhelming attraction for her, and she stared up at him, willing him to kiss her.

When he didn't move, but continued to search her features for something, some elusive answer she would have given him willingly had she but known what he asked of her, she deliberately broke the spell. "Maybe . . . maybe we'd better be getting back to the hotel," she whispered in a parody of her usual assured tones.

"Maybe you're right," he agreed huskily, his eyes still moving relentlessly over her hair, her lips, her body. "Yes, let's go now, before I . . ."

To her acute disappointment, he turned her in the direction they had come and all too soon, with only one yearning, backward glance at the spectacle of moonlight on a tranquil sea, she allowed herself to be ushered into another taxi.

There was a message at the desk that there had been two calls for Mr. McCloud, and Frances wondered sinkingly if perhaps Katherine wanted to see him again tonight.

Don't let it be that, she prayed silently. Don't let him leave me now, not now that the practical, independent Frances has finally surrendered to this island magic. It had been inevitable once they began this trip; she knew that, only it had been hard to accept the fact that, come what may, tonight she was going to become Mrs. Cabel McCloud in fact as well as in name.

With no thought for the ashes of tomorrow, she allowed the flame to leap up the moment Cabel closed the door behind them. He touched her cheek . . . only touched it lightly, but it was enough to set off the conflagration that had been smouldering for so long. His kiss was a tender coercion of her drunken senses, and then it deepened, as if he were setting his brand on her for all time. He lifted his head and smiled at her response, his eyes heavy-lidded and unnaturally dark, and when he led her to the bedroom and began unfastening the hook and eye at the back of her neck, sliding the long zipper down to slip his hands in along her sides, she leaned back against him, tremulously aware of his aroused state.

Somehow, in a slow, sensuous sequence that never seemed quite real, they managed to move to the bed, with her gown falling to the floor, followed by Cabel's white linen suit and blue silk shirt. He drew her down beside him, his eyes lit from within with a passion that licked at her nerves like raw, greedy flames.

"Reach the light, darling," she whispered, captive under the weight of him.

"I want to see you while I'm making love to you. I want to watch those jade-green eyes of yours melt when I touch you . . . here and here." He followed his words with small kisses, lighting butterfly soft on her body as she trembled helplessly. "Touch me, darling," he groaned, taking her hands and moving them to his chest.

Her fingers tangled in the crisp hair and followed it as it swirled down the flat of his abdomen. He groaned in pleasure. Instinct guided her—pure, wanton instinct born of loving the man until she was well-nigh distraught with it.

"God, how did you learn to please a man like that?" he ground out, his eyes glowing with a metallic hardness as the tendons of his neck held his head away from her. "It kills me to think about it," he groaned.

She was in no fit condition to think, much less talk, but as the meaning of his words gradually seeped into her mind, Frances grew still. Her eyes were enormous troubled pools as reason struggled with pure animal passion. She whispered almost inaudibly, "But I never learned, Cabel . . . I . . . I only *know*."

As if the sound of her voice ripped away the last shred of his control, he moved over her, guiding her pliant body to accept him and then his sudden look of shock, her soft cry, like a wounded bird—all were caught up in the maelstrom of irreversible passion. If there was a new gentleness in the way he held her, they were both beyond knowing it, beyond knowing anything but the spinning free-fall through space that left them both half-unconscious in each other's arms.

Hours later, it was the intrusion of the phone that brought her awake. She moved and felt an aching awareness of her body, and beside her Cabel stirred.

"Mmmm, darling?" he murmured, reaching for her, but then came the shrill summons again and he turned with a muffled oath and lifted the receiver.

Frances, her eyes devouring him hungrily, saw the sudden stiffness in his shoulders, and then the shutters that came down over his eyes hid his feelings from her completely. His voice, though, when he spoke roughly into the phone, made her know he was shocked.

"How did you know . . . No! I can't see you now . . . Alright, then . . . yes. Half an hour."

She waited. It was all too new to her and she couldn't break through the barrier he had erected to ask what was wrong, but she willed him to tell her, not to shut her out . . . not after last night.

"I have to go out," he said tersely, throwing aside the sheet to stride across the floor.

He was naked and the sight of his powerful, beautiful body brought a weakness to the center of her body. "Alone?" she asked tentatively.

"Yes."

While he showered, Frances curled up into a defensive ball and tried to hold onto a fragment of the magic of her wedding night, but it was no use. Cabel had closed her out as effectively as if she had been back in her little house on the river, instead of on this bewitching island with him.

She pretended to be asleep when he emerged from the bathroom and whether or not he was convinced, it obviously suited him to go along with the deception. He closed the door softly behind him. She felt herself collapse and realized she had been holding herself in a frozen attitude for so long she could barely move.

The whole time she was soaking in her bath, she was wondering if Katherine had summoned him for some personal reason of her own. Someone *had* to see him . . . immediately. Could it be Tony? Had marriage number four—or was it five?—dissolved right under their very noses?

There was no point in second-guessing. Cabel was no stranger here in the Bahamas and it could be anyone. He had made several calls earlier, and come to think of it, there were those two calls last night while they were out. Perhaps it was business.

Yes, that was it! It was business and Cabel didn't want to allow business to interfere with their newly established intimacy. She had not imagined the tenderness last night when he had discovered that she wasn't as experienced as she had led him to believe. At the time, there had been no turning back, not for either of them. But in retrospect, she saw again that sudden stunned expression, felt again the almost cradling tenderness that had immediately been swept away on waves of white-hot flames.

She had dressed in a sleeveless green linen and was considering ordering herself something to eat when there came a soft tap on her door. She answered it, opening it to see Katherine Beal standing there in a flawlessly designed steel-gray silk that could have only come from Paris.

"Where's Cabel?" his mother asked, glancing into the suite.

Confused, Frances stood back to allow her to enter. "Why . . . I thought he might be with you," she said.

"Not since last night, but that's better still." The older woman seemed to have made up her mind about something. She turned to Frances and said, "Frances, I need to talk to you . . . alone. Can we go somewhere where we won't be disturbed?"

Chapter Ten

There was plenty of time on the long, lonely flight home to dwell on the few hours after she had opened the door to the sad, embittered woman. Katherine had come in and paced like a small, highly strung animal until Frances asked her if she'd care for some coffee.

She had turned about at that, and asked point-blank, "Frances, do you love my son?"

Subterfuge was out of the question. There had been such a world of feeling behind the half-dozen words that Frances could only nod slowly. "Yes. For my sins, I'm afraid I do."

The floodgates were down then. Katherine had not minced words in telling Frances about the almost unbearably happy days of her marriage, when she had been all of eighteen. "Mac . . . Cabe's father, was almost twenty years older than I was, already well-established. He had just moved into a big house on Park Ridge with all his family's things. . . . My own people had nothing, you understand. There were his offices in the Loop, all his friends and business acquaintances who had known him long before I had."

She broke off to light a cigarette and Frances remained silent, sensing her need to unburden herself.

"I was just too damned young and ignorant to know what was good for me!" she cried in a voice that was stripped of everything but pain. "I loved that man more than anything on earth, more than I did my own child, but I didn't have sense enough to realize it until it was too late."

After the brittle silence had stretched too far, Frances prompted softly, "What happened?"

Blinking as if she had just returned from a long trip back in time, Katherine had spelled out an all too common tale of a busy husband and a bored wife, tied to a home and a child too soon, afraid she was missing out on all the more glamorous things life could offer. "God, what did I care that the wretched china was museum quality, that the family predated the Revolution? Along came a beautiful, fast-talking actor with an eye to the main chance and I ran off without one backward look—all set to live a glamorous life in Beverly Hills!"

Only the glamorous life had never materialized, and poor Katherine had gone from disillusion to disillusion, ending with the present husband who had married her for the money Cabel's father had settled on her when they had been married. It had been skillfully invested and now paid her a more than generous allowance, but it had not brought happiness.

"Frances, all I ask is that you love my son with every beat of your heart. Don't do to him what I did to his father, or I don't think I can stand it." Those tragic eyes, so like Cabel's, had bored into Frances's very soul; even now, she couldn't forget them, nor the careless words a few moments later that had shattered any chance for her own marriage.

"Are you expecting Cabe back soon?" Katherine had asked, stubbing out another cigarette in the overflowing ashtray.

"I really don't know. He got a call and had to go out. Business, I suppose."

"Oh, that would be the Dawson woman," Katherine had said carelessly. "She called me after I got in last night, said Cabe's secretary had given her my phone number. I told her where he was staying. Just like his father; business twenty-four hours a day, seven days a week."

By the time Frances reached Atlanta, things began to take on a grayness that matched her mood. There was little to do but think, for the elderly man beside her slept the whole way, snoring occasionally, then rousing to shuffle his feet, smack his lips, and doze off again.

At Raleigh-Durham, she was faced with a dilemma; they had come in Cabel's car and he had the keys. But she called Helen Aurther who came and fetched her and, after one long, measuring look, began chattering about a grad student, female, who was going to move into Milo's room for the term.

"You're sure you don't want me to come in with you?" Helen pressed on the porch of the small house by the river. "I could call Jerrold and tell him where I am."

"Thanks, Aunt Helen, but it's really not necessary. It's been so long since I've had a minute to relax. I'm going to heat some soup, make a pot of coffee, and sleep until Tuesday morning."

"And Cabel?"

"He'll be along tomorrow night. We went to see his mother, you know, and he decided to stay on for another day." She had thought it all out, the excuses that would prevent any questioning until things were settled and the split was irrevocably made.

After only two days the house had that unused feeling, but of course there had also been the two days she'd stayed at Cabel's house before she left. Shrugging off her coat, she reached for the thermostat and then decided that she needed the psychological boost of a blazing fire tonight. So she put a match to the logs that had been laid in the wood stove over a month before.

Under her beige coat, she was still wearing the green linen dress she had put on first thing this morning. . . . Was it only this morning? Lord, it seemed two lifetimes ago! Funny how a mind refused to stretch over long distances sometimes. In Nassau, Bynum hadn't seemed quite real; and now here in Bynum, Nassau was a figment of her imagination.

But would a figment of her imagination cause such a very real pain in her heart? Would the dull ache in her mind, the persistent refusal to dredge up certain memories result from a figment of her imagination?

Turning her face away from the answer, she put on a pot of coffee and set a pan of canned soup on the wood stove to heat, adding another log to the fat blaze inside the chubby little iron stove before running herself a bath. Outside, the rain drummed down on her tin roof as though it would never end.

* * *

Before going to bed, she sat huddled up in her comfortable chair, snug in a long-sleeved, high-necked nightgown of rose-sprigged flannel, and stared at the untouched cup of coffee in her hands. The soup had been inedible, cooked down on the roaring fire to a thick, ambiguous concentrate under a shiny skin that sagged over the top. She put it aside for Tripod.

Must remember to pick her up tomorrow . . . or the next day. Or the next. She sniffed and hoped she wasn't coming down with a cold. Her unfocused thoughts picked up the homey smell of soup, coffee, and rich pine wood that had replaced the empty-house atmosphere. This was her home, after all. This was the real world, the autumn rain that flailed the stoic pines and cedars and whipped the bare branches of the ailanthus and the redbud. Outside, the red hills were washing down to thicken the river, and the red and yellow leaves that had hung on until now would be plastering her white Aspen tomorrow when the sun came out again. If the sun came out again.

Oh, Lord, I'm getting maudlin! She got up and stirred herself to heat a cup of milk, pouring the coffee down the drain in disgust. One thing she didn't need was another sleepless night, and on the heels of that thought came another: there'd be nobody to keep her awake tonight, at least.

Her bed was a lonely place, which was ridiculous, considering that she had slept alone all her life but for that one night. Finally, the rain on the roof took effect, and she surrendered to an emotional exhaustion that even surpassed her physical tiredness.

* * *

The rain had let up to a dispirited drizzle when she opened her eyes to the darkness again. For several minutes she lay there, half-asleep, and wondered what had aroused her. Then it came to her.

"Oh, my Lord, no!" she whispered, sliding her feet out of bed and feeling her way to the door.

The smoke in the living room was thick enough to gag her. She stepped back into her bedroom and slammed the door, stunned with a sense of disbelief. It couldn't be happening. It simply couldn't! Hard on the heels of her discovery, she was galvanized into action by the sound of something falling overhead, and she opened the door and peered out to see the terrifying glow that grew brighter even as she watched. With no thought except to get out, she threw open the window and leaned out. It wasn't more than six feet. The rain beat on her head and in a moment of pure, blind panic, she dashed back across the room and snatched the watercolor off her wall and then grabbed her purse, thinking not of her money, but of the jade ring she had tucked into the handkerchief in one compartment before leaving Nassau.

Once on the ground, she backed off, wide-eyed and dazed, and saw the first flicker of flames lick up her chimney. She turned with a small, inarticulate cry and ran up the hill to the dark house that loomed against the darker trees. She still had the key in her purse, not that she had even thought of that until she actually stood at the door, but she let herself inside with trembling hands and hurried to the phone to summon the fire department.

The firemen had gone, having come too late to do more than watch the roof settle into the foundation.

Frances had stood outside and watched, in spite of all the efforts to make her go back inside Cabel's house. Now she waited for Patsy to come and get her. She was wet and her gown flapped disconsolately about her legs, but she wasn't even aware of the fact that she was gray with soot and smoke, that she was shivering with a fine tremor that had as much to do with nerves as with the fact that she had been standing outside in her sodden nightgown for more than an hour. Now she sat alone in the hallway of Cabel's house, unaware of the chill of the rooms, oblivious to anything except relief that Tripod wasn't there when the fire started.

The watercolor she had rescued was propped outdoors in the rain against the walnut tree that had stood halfway between the two houses . . . only now there was only the one.

Shock absorbed the worst of the pain, leaving only numbness behind it. When she saw the sweep of headlights strike the front door, shattering rainbows as it crossed the beveled edges of the decorative glass panels, she lifted her head and waited patiently. Only the sound of the slamming car door and the feet that pounded up the stairs roused her out of her protective shell of apathy, and she jumped up with a small cry and ran forward to throw herself into Patsy's comforting arms.

Only it wasn't Patsy who stood there, blocking out the gray curtain of rain, filling the doorway and filling her heart to overflowing. Momentum had carried her forward, checking her only when it was too late, and Cabel wrapped her in his arms with a crippling strength, wringing her to him as he repeated her name over and over.

It didn't occur to her to wonder how he knew; she simply let him hold her, let him lift her in his arms

177

and climb the stairs with her to lower her onto his bed and wrap her in a down-filled comforter.

"Cabel," she whispered hoarsely, holding up a grimy wrist to twist it slowly before her bewildered eyes, "I'm dirty. I'm filthy, Cabel. You shouldn't get your nice clean bed all wet and dirty."

"Shut up, precious," he growled, stepping into the hallway long enough to turn on the furnace in the basement. He peeled off the light raincoat he wore and tossed it aside, returning to study her face with grave concern. "I'm going to run you a hot bath and bring you something to drink. Don't move from here until I get back, do you understand?"

She blinked at him from the thick pillow. "You don't need to do that, Cabel. Mama's coming for me. She'll take care of everything." Her voice was small, but very calm and it held an almost dreamlike quality that brought a quick expression of pain to the man's narrowed eyes.

"Stay here," he repeated tersely, disappearing into the large, old-fashioned bathroom with its enormous porcelain and golden oak bathtub. He left the room and she heard his feet take the stairs two at a time. Then she allowed her mind to drift again, unwilling to reach for reality until she had someone to hold onto.

Cabel was back almost immediately with the brandy. He poured her a stiff dose and then watched while she forced it down, not protesting, but choking slightly. He took the glass from her unresisting fingers, then lifted her, and began stripping off the ruined gown. "God, you're like ice!" he muttered, his voice hardly recognizable as he stood her naked on her feet and then swept her up and carried her the few feet to lower her into the steamy water.

"Ouch! That's hot," she wailed, rousing slightly

for the first time as something from the outside world impinged on her inner haven.

"Good! It's going to take more than hot water to get you clean again. You look like a chimney sweep!" He soaped the cloth and went to work and suddenly, it was as if her vision cleared and she sat up and snatched the washcloth from his hand.

"Get out of here! You have no business in here while I'm bathing!" she protested angrily, sliding down under the water that was already beginning to look slightly gray.

By the time she had run two tubs of water and scoured herself until her skin was an angry red, she heard sounds coming from the adjoining room that announced Patsy's arrival. She climbed out, wrinkling her nose at the messy ring she was leaving and patted herself dry with one of Cabel's enormous wraparound towels, tucking another over her hair. Then, seeing that there was nothing else to wear, she let herself out of the steamy atmosphere into the comparative chill of the bedroom and there her mother greeted her with a small cry.

"Mama, it's all right," she crooned over and over to the weeping woman. Cabel leaned against the bedroom fireplace, cold and dark, she saw thankfully, and watched as she brought her mother to a state of acceptance. "Look, the house was insured and I certainly didn't have all that much tied up in furnishings. My cat was with Margaret, so I haven't really lost anything that can't be replaced." She forced a small, brittle laugh as Patsy backed away, fumbling for a handkerchief. "Besides, the kitchen was impossible. I'd never have been able to fit a decent cabinet in there. This way I can plan everything the way I want it. After all," she concluded, "the land's still mine."

"Well, all right, Fancey, but I'm sure I don't know how you can take everything so calmly. If it were me, I'd be all to pieces!"

"Don't worry about Fancey, Mrs. Harris," Cabel broke in, moving forward with a purposeful air now. He picked up Patsy's coat and held it for her and she had no choice but to slide her plump arms into the sleeves.

"Oh, but . . ." she began, twisting to cast a questioning look up at Cabel.

"I'll just see you out, Patsy," he told her firmly. "I think Fancey needs an early night . . . good Lord, it's broad daylight, isn't it?" He left with an arm over the older woman's shoulder, and Frances stared at the door he had closed deliberately behind him. It was as if he had spoken the words aloud: Stay here. I'm not finished with you.

She stayed because there was little else she could do, other than run after Patsy and insist on going with her. She knew her days as her mother's daughter were at an end in that sense. It didn't bear dwelling on, the options still open to her, and she could only wait, her mind drifting off into that self-protective cocoon again, until she heard her husband's firm, relentless tread coming back to her.

Instead of coming to her immediately, he crossed to the walnut highboy—one that must have been in his family for generations, she now realized—and lifted out a navy blue silk pajama shirt that looked as if it had never been worn, which was no less than the truth.

"Put it on," he ordered evenly.

She turned her back and let the towel slip while she eased her arms into the luxurious comfort. Lord knows, there was little need for modesty now, not after he had dumped her into the tub and scrubbed her filthy body. Nevertheless, she buttoned the last button before turning to him again, to wait expectantly for whatever was to come next. Whether it was to be recriminations for running out on him, or explanations for the breakup of their marriage, or simply condolences on the loss of her house, she was prepared to face it. Time and distance had taught her that she could turn away from truths too painful to accept. It didn't cure anything, but it bought time for the healing process to begin.

"Well?" he prompted, throwing her into a state of minor confusion. The ball was in his court, or at least she had tossed it there when she walked out on him, whether he picked it up or not.

"Well?" she echoed numbly. She was seated on the edge of the bed, her shoulders held rigidly and her hands clasped in her lap. Outside, the watery sun was beginning to reveal the devastation of the night, but she didn't look to the window. She kept her eyes focused on the tall, grim-faced man who stood leaning against the mantel, not sparing her with his raking scrutiny.

"All right, I'll go first, but in that case, you're not to speak until I give you permission," he said implacably.

Her chin lifted as some of the sparkle returned to her shadowed eyes. "Now, just a minute, there, McCloud, I . . ."

"Quiet!"

She subsided, clenching her fingers until her broken nails bit into her palms. Then she lowered her chin again and closed her eyes. He began to speak and then he stopped abruptly.

Her eyes flew open and as she stared at him in consternation, taking in the lined grayness of his face, the stubble on his aggressive jaw, she saw his eyes grow suspiciously bright and with an oath that was torn from him roughly, he crossed to where she sat meekly and gathered her up into his arms.

"Oh, Christ, Frances, you don't know what you're doing to me!" he groaned into her damp hair. His hands were biting into her flesh, holding her so closely that she could feel the hardness of his chest, the edge of his rib cage bruising the softness of her tender breasts.

"Cabel," she protested, trying frantically to prevent herself from simply accepting his comforting sympathy as a substitute for what she could never have.

He lifted his head slightly to stare down at her, and she thought wonderingly that from the expression in his eyes, her loss had hurt him even more then it had her. She reached up and traced the deeply chiseled line from his nose to the corner of his mouth with an unsteady finger.

"Cabel?" she whispered. "It's all right. I can rebuild after awhile, or . . . or even let you buy my land, if you want to clear it off, and I'll relocate somewhere else." She looked at him hopefully, not allowing herself to think of the coming separation. She had grown skilled at separating her feelings from her mind lately, through trying to spare herself unbearable pain.

Space between them widened, allowing the coolness of the morning air to flow between them and he turned away from her, leaning his arms on his thighs as he stared at the faded rug beneath his feet.

Clearing her throat of the miserable lump that seemed to have lodged there permanently, Frances asked, "Is that what you want, Cabel?"

"What I want!" The gray face that turned to stare with a twisted grimace bore little resemblance to the sardonic, sophisticated man she had married. "Shall I tell you what I want then, Frances? Shall I hand you a laugh? You could use one about now." His biting words cut through her sensitivity like a serrated blade. "I *want* . . . you, Frances. Not to run my household, not to play hostess to some unimportant business connection, but to be a part of my life, a part of *me* . . . the part that was missing all my life, only I was too damned stupid to know it." He continued to stare at her as if expecting her to join him in the joke, but she could no more laugh than she could fly!

Defenses were flung up helter-skelter as she silently warned herself not to walk blindly into another trap.

"Frances? Don't you see the joke? It's funny, girl . . . it's hilarious. It only started sinking in when I discovered you were gone, but I had plenty of time on the way home to enjoy the fine irony of it."

He was torturing himself and it was tearing her apart. She laid a hand on his arm and he flinched as if her touch were electric. "Cabel," she insisted, reaching for him again and grasping one of the fists that rested on his taut, muscular thigh. "Cabel, I don't know what you're getting at exactly, but if it makes it any easier, I want you to know that . . . that . . ." Here came the hard part. "I love you."

She might just as well have struck him, for the response she got. He stared at her with dark, glittering eyes, his mouth even harder than before. "Is this your idea of a punch line? As much as I admire your sense of humor, girl, I . . ."

"Cabel, damn it, I love you!" she shouted, shaking his fist in both her hands. "If you're going to be so pigheaded about it, I'll just . . ."

She got no further, nor did she know what she would have done if he hadn't flung her back on the bed and made further words impossible. He was kissing her as if kissing were a language that extended beyond the realm of mere words. She discovered that it was just that as his searching, seeking tongue, his hands and his lips and every part of his body told her of an aching need that went far beyond all reason.

Somewhere along the way, his shirt, the black knit that still smelled of the islands and of Cabel, himself, had come off, and the outsized pajama top she wore fell by the wayside as he made love to her with all the tenderness imaginable. When the rest of his clothes followed the shirt, he led her into another world, a world of the senses where he proved himself a knowledgeable guide and she could only cling to him and trust him to bring her back safely to earth.

It was a long, long way down, but eventually they lay satiated in each other's arms. "Fancey?" he whispered, his voice still unsteady as the surging of his heart slowly subsided. "Say it again."

"I love you, Cabel." She was beyond being coy, beyond pretending, even though she was still uncertain just how the miracle had come about.

"Always?"

"And beyond that, darling. Always is too specific for the love I have for you. It spells out limits and there are none."

With his lips traveling along the line of her still damp hair, he began to tell her of his feelings. "I guess you're never so vulnerable as when you think you know it all. I knew all about women when I met you. Knew exactly what I wanted from them and how to get that and nothing more . . . how to be a real bastard, I suppose."

She was silent, knowing that the basis of his feelings went back a long way.

"When you came along . . . in a manner that couldn't be overlooked, I might add, I told myself you were a new challenge. At that time, I honestly don't know what I wanted from you. I enjoyed our fights. Like pepper in the chowder," he grinned down at her, touching one of her eyelids with the tip of his tongue. "But then I began to be bored with all the others. Not only that, you imp of the devil, but I found my . . . ah . . . prowess as a lover suffering drastically. When the setting was right, the mood, the timing, everything perfect, I'd see your impudent eyes flashing green fire at me and hear your crusty remarks, as if you were standing there in the background passing judgment. I can tell you, you played hell with my love life!"

"Oh, Cabe, I didn't," she gurgled, her imagination filling in the delightfully amusing details. "But you kept on . . . I mean, Olivia kept on . . ."

"Hush, darling. I don't want that conniving female to cause us any more trouble, so let me just say that Olivia's . . . uh . . . charms had begun to pale shortly after I met you, but I couldn't just drop all my social life and sit up here on the hill while you went prancing out with those Irishmen. In fact, if you want the whole truth, I wasn't above trying to make you jealous," he admitted, "hoping I could make a dent in that cast-iron armor plate you wore."

"Oh, you made a dent all right! I could have crowned you with a king-sized chunk of it more than once," she teased, allowing her fingers to play through the crisp curls on his chest. "Did you actually offer that woman my jade ring before you . . ."

"Listen, and get this straight! I never offered any

woman more than a first-class dinner and a good time. I bought that ring because you told me about your interest in the Orient and because it's the color of your eyes just before you laugh aloud . . . oh, yes, they change color and I'm well aware of every single shade. Want to know what my favorite is?" He grinned down at her audaciously.

"I'm afraid to ask," she ventured, discovering new delights as she allowed her hands to grow bolder.

"When they begin to grow darker and darker as the pupil swallows up all but a tiny rim of green . . . the way they're beginning to do right now," he growled, turning over to press her against the mattress. "Shall I make the last bit of green disappear?"

She held off the inevitable with one slender hand as she persisted, "Then you didn't give Olivia that sapphire necklace?"

"Give her . . . Good Lord, Frances, do I look like that sort of a fool? Olivia sells the stuff. She works at one of the better jewelry stores and no, for your information, my precious little porcupine, I did not buy your ring from Olivia. Now, will you shut up and allow me to get on with the rest of our life?"

Silhouette **Romance**

15-Day Free Trial Offer
6 Silhouette Romances

6 Silhouette Romances, free for 15 days! We'll send you 6 new Silhouette Romances to keep for 15 days, absolutely free! If you decide not to keep them, send them back to us. You pay nothing.

Free Home Delivery. But if you enjoy them as much as we think you will, keep them by paying the invoice enclosed with your free trial shipment. We'll pay all shipping and handling charges. You get the convenience of Home Delivery and we pay the postage and handling charge each month.

Don't miss a copy. The Silhouette Book Club is the way to make sure you'll be able to receive every new romance we publish before they're sold out. There is no minimum number of books to buy and you can cancel at any time.

Silhouette Romance

IT'S YOUR OWN SPECIAL TIME

Contemporary romances for today's women.
Each month, six very special love stories will be yours
from SILHOUETTE. Look for them wherever books are sold
or order now from the coupon below.

$1.50 each

Hampson	☐ 1	☐ 4	☐ 16	☐ 27		Browning	☐ 12	☐ 38	☐ 53	☐ 73
	☐ 28	☐ 40	☐ 52	☐ 64	☐ 94		☐ 93			
Stanford	☐ 6	☐ 25	☐ 35	☐ 46		Michaels	☐ 15	☐ 32	☐ 61	☐ 87
	☐ 58	☐ 88				John	☐ 17	☐ 34	☐ 57	☐ 85
Hastings	☐ 13	☐ 26	☐ 44	☐ 67		Beckman	☐ 8	☐ 37	☐ 54	☐ 72
Vitek	☐ 33	☐ 47	☐ 66	☐ 84			☐ 96			

$1.50 each

☐ 5 Goforth	☐ 29 Wildman	☐ 56 Trent	☐ 79 Halldorson
☐ 7 Lewis	☐ 30 Dixon	☐ 59 Vernon	☐ 80 Stephens
☐ 9 Wilson	☐ 31 Halldorson	☐ 60 Hill	☐ 81 Roberts
☐ 10 Caine	☐ 36 McKay	☐ 62 Hallston	☐ 82 Dailey
☐ 11 Vernon	☐ 39 Sinclair	☐ 63 Brent	☐ 83 Halston
☐ 14 Oliver	☐ 41 Owen	☐ 69 St. George	☐ 86 Adams
☐ 19 Thornton	☐ 42 Powers	☐ 70 Afton Bonds	☐ 89 James
☐ 20 Fulford	☐ 43 Robb	☐ 71 Ripy	☐ 90 Major
☐ 21 Richards	☐ 45 Carroll	☐ 74 Trent	☐ 92 McKay
☐ 22 Stephens	☐ 48 Wildman	☐ 75 Carroll	☐ 95 Wisdom
☐ 23 Edwards	☐ 49 Wisdom	☐ 76 Hardy	☐ 97 Clay
☐ 24 Healy	☐ 50 Scott	☐ 77 Cork	☐ 98 St. George
	☐ 55 Ladame	☐ 78 Oliver	☐ 99 Camp

$1.75 each

☐ 100 Stanford	☐ 105 Eden	☐ 110 Trent	☐ 115 John
☐ 101 Hardy	☐ 106 Dailey	☐ 111 South	☐ 116 Lindley
☐ 102 Hastings	☐ 107 Bright	☐ 112 Stanford	☐ 117 Scott
☐ 103 Cork	☐ 108 Hampson	☐ 113 Browning	☐ 118 Dailey
☐ 104 Vitek	☐ 109 Vernon	☐ 114 Michaels	☐ 119 Hampson

$1.75 each

Silhouette Desire
15-Day Trial Offer
A new romance series
that explores
contemporary relationships
in exciting detail

Four Silhouette Desire romances, free for 15 days!
We'll send you four new Silhouette Desire romances
to look over for 15 days, absolutely free! If you decide
not to keep the books, return them and owe nothing.

Four books a month, free home delivery. If you like
Silhouette Desire romances as much as we think you
will, keep them and return your payment with the
invoice. Then we will send you four new books every
month to preview, just as soon as they are published.
You pay only for the books you decide to keep, and
you never pay postage and handling.

Silhouette Romance

Coming next month from
Silhouette Romances

Dreams From The Past by Linda Wisdom

Kelly went to Australia to fulfill a promise to her father, to see the woman he had first loved, Maureen Cassidy. How could she have known that in Maureen's son Jake she would find a love to last forever?

A Silver Nutmeg by Elizabeth Hunter

Judi Duggan had gone to Spain to design and stitch the trappings for the Arnalte family chapel. She didn't plan to meet the handsome Don—and she certainly didn't plan to fall in love!

Moonlight And Memories by Eleni Carr

Helen had dreamed of a chance to spend the summer in Greece. But the presence of deep, mysterious Demetrios Criades unsettled her. Could she unlock the passions hidden in the chambers of his heart?

Lover Come Back by Joanna Scott

One night of love made her his forever, bound by memory—and a child. Linda tried to escape, but how could she resist this master of the dangerous game of hearts?

A Treasure Of Love by Margaret Ripy

From the moment she met him, Marnie Stevens regretted signing on as Damon Wilson's underwater photographer. But with a will as steely as his penetrating gray eyes, he demanded fulfillment of the contract—in every way!

Lady Moon by Heather Hill

Maggie Jordan had come to the English countryside to restore Deane Park—a vast, Georgian estate. But after meeting its aristocratic owner, she realized the real challenge would be the man, not the job!

READERS' COMMENTS ON SILHOUETTE ROMANCES:

"I would like to congratulate you on the most wonderful books I've had the pleasure of reading. They are a tremendous joy to those of us who have yet to meet the man of our dreams. From reading your books I quite truly believe that he will some-day appear before me like a prince!"

—L.L.*, Hollandale, MS

"Your books are great, wholesome fiction, always with an upbeat, happy ending. Thank you."

—M.D., Massena, NY

"My boyfriend always teases me about Silhouette Books. He asks me, how's my love life and natu-rally I say terrific, but I tell him that there is always room for a little more romance from Sil-houette."

—F.N., Ontario, Canada

"I would like to sincerely express my gratitude to you and your staff for bringing the pleasure of your publications to my attention. Your books are well written, mature and very contemporary."

—D.D., Staten Island, NY

*names available on request